Party M

Color code for each party member for easy cross referencing

Write names and descriptions of key NPCs on the left page.

Relations

Character

Name _____

Class / Race _____

Description _____

_____

_____

_____

_____

Motivations _____

_____

_____

Vocation _____

Trade _____

Hobbies _____

Strengths _____

Faults/Weaknesses _____

Notes _____

_____

_____

_____

Relations

Character

Name _____

Class / Race _____

Description _____

_____

_____

_____

_____

Motivations _____

_____

_____

_____

Vocation _____

Trade _____

Hobbies _____

Strengths _____

Faults/Weaknesses _____

Notes _____

_____

_____

_____

Relations

Character

Name _____

Class / Race _____

Description _____

_____

_____

_____

_____

Motivations _____

_____

_____

_____

Vocation _____

Trade _____

Hobbies _____

Strengths _____

Faults/Weaknesses _____

Notes _____

_____

_____

_____

Relations

Character

Name _____

Class / Race _____

Description _____

_____

_____

_____

_____

Motivations _____

_____

_____

Vocation _____

Trade _____

Hobbies _____

Strengths _____

Faults/Weaknesses _____

Notes _____

_____

_____

Relations

Character

Name _____

Class / Race _____

Description _____

_____

_____

_____

Motivations _____

_____

_____

Vocation _____

Trade _____

Hobbies _____

Strengths _____

Faults/Weaknesses _____

Notes _____

_____

_____

Relations

Character

Name _____

Class / Race _____

Description _____

_____

_____

_____

Motivations _____

_____

_____

Vocation _____

Trade _____

Hobbies _____

Strengths _____

Faults/Weaknesses _____

Notes _____

_____

_____

Relations

Character

Name _____

Class / Race _____

Description _____

_____

_____

_____

_____

Motivations _____

_____

_____

Vocation _____

Trade _____

Hobbies _____

Strengths _____

Faults/Weaknesses _____

Notes _____

_____

_____

Relations

Character

Name

Class / Race

Description

Motivations

Vocation

Trade

Hobbies

Strengths

Faults/Weaknesses

Notes

Relations

Character

Name _____

Class / Race _____

Description _____

_____

_____

_____

_____

Motivations _____

_____

_____

_____

Vocation _____

Trade _____

Hobbies _____

Strengths _____

Faults/Weaknesses _____

Notes _____

_____

_____

Relations

Character

Name _____

Class / Race _____

Description _____

_____

_____

_____

_____

Motivations _____

_____

_____

_____

Vocation _____

Trade _____

Hobbies _____

Strengths _____

Faults/Weaknesses _____

Notes _____

_____

_____

_____

Relations

Character

Name _____

Class / Race _____

Description _____

_____

_____

_____

Motivations _____

_____

_____

Vocation _____

Trade _____

Hobbies _____

Strengths _____

Faults/Weaknesses _____

Notes _____

_____

_____

Relations

Character

Name _____

Class / Race _____

Description _____

_____

_____

_____

_____

Motivations _____

_____

_____

Vocation _____

Trade _____

Hobbies _____

Strengths _____

Faults/Weaknesses _____

Notes _____

_____

_____

Party Backstory Generator

This book is a Party Backstory Generator (PBG) and campaign pre-quel/map creator. It allows your party to quickly and randomly establish who they are, what tensions and motivations exist, and how that can enrich your campaign. The map your players will collaboratively create will become a living game board as well. It can also serve as a drop table that will spawn epic clashes and crush emotional alliances.

This book can also act as a nonlinear storytelling device. As your main campaign develops, you can take a break from it and go back in time and play a one-shot that can both fill in backstory and create meaning within your campaign or adventure. I created this book with this nonlinear fiction device in mind.

The PBG is not for individual character development—there are plenty of great resources that already do that. This book quickly builds relationships between characters to create meaningful alliances and tensions. You will often be prompted to "Choose two characters..." (always meaning Playable Characters or PCs) and this will bond two players together in ways you and they can manipulate. Remember, whenever "character(s)" is mentioned in the book, it is meant as player's character. Non-playable characters are typically marked as NPCs.

The only pages your players can see and fill out are the blank map pages (inside covers and thick end paper) and the Relation/Character pages in the beginning of the book. The rest of the book including the dice lists and Location/Event and other pages are for the game master (GM) only.

You should not begin this process with any sort of agenda other than letting your players get invented in your world. Your players will create this part of their world collaboratively with your guidance. In order for them to have the most fun, let them take ownership of the experience without compromising your overall narrative or campaign. You might want to set up restrictions up front instead of saying "no" over and over as game-breaking ideas are introduced. For instance, you can say, "So listen, this is a low fantasy setting so magic is scarce and there are no strange classes." Or "Keep in mind there's very little edible vegetation here and the water is somewhat toxic." This way your players won't be silently creating their world and waiting to speak only to have you shoot their idea down. Be clear about what can and cannot exist in this backstory.

This book is not meant to be filled in all at once in one session. Take your time. Go back to it between game nights as a group and fill in more as your campaign develops. This book can function as a fun "off night" where the group comes together and creates meaningful backstory. I suggest never adding to or editing this book without the entire group present. It's meant to be an experience for the party—a living document that everyone shares. Treat this book like a living document that will help your players bond as characters.

This book is also not meant to replace anything in your campaign that should not be replaced. If you already have a town or environment in mind, maybe the town/city created by this book existed before the current setting. This book is meant to be as flexible as possible—throw out what you don't need and adapt as you see fit. Some randomly generated content might not fit your narrative at all. Feel free to scrap it and roll again if necessary.

When appropriate, it can be useful to weave the randomly generated relations and locations together, making some NPCs related or reliant on one another or having properties owned by the same person.

Note, the Drop Slide tables are in the center of the book and break one section of the text. We wanted those tables to be as close to the middle as possible for ease of use (holding the book in one hand).

Randomly Generated Backstory

This section will allow you to create backstory quickly with a few dice rolls. The book is divided into two halves: the left has randomly generated options for building your party's backstory and the right has fillable pages to keep track of that content. Don't repeat occurrences. If a character rolls the same outcome as another character, they will roll again until a different outcome is generated.

The 12 boxes on the right side of the pages are your character markers. Assign a color or symbol to each playable character or important non-playable character. Whenever an important conflict or alliance occurs, color/mark that box so you can cross reference who it effects. Use the system that makes the most sense for your story. Before committing to a system, you might want to give it a try on scrap paper.

Map

The front inside cover and end paper are meant for your players/characters to draw their town/city map or area where they are from. If you want to use a separate piece of paper (as large as you want), you definitely can. I prefer a larger separate map because its easier for players to draw on. When using the drop tables, a larger map is also more fun to roll on. If you decide to use a separate larger map for the overall area, this frees your players up to use the front of the book to draw additional locations and more detailed versions of their property. And it allows more than one person to draw/write at the same time.

The map in the front of the book (or separate poster/paper) is a large over-world map so structures should be very small. Imagine that the map space can take up the size of a large town or city with surrounding terrain: woods, mountains, or whatever your world allows. For example, if you're using a large piece of paper or pasteboard that's 24 inches by 36 inches, that should probably represent 2 x 3 miles.

This isn't the overall world; you probably have a separate map for that. This is meant for the party to draw where they came from. If they are from the same town or city, they will draw that. If they are from the same area/country, they will draw that with indicators showing where each character is from. Roll for initiative and let the highest rolling character draw for one minute, explaining where their character is from and as much of their backstory as they wish to reveal. It's important to give them enough time to bring their imagination to the collaborative narrative. The next player/character in initiative order draws on the map and does the same. Allow each player/character to feel invested in what they shared and/or drew.

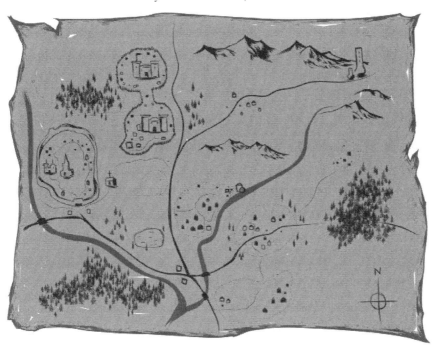

This setup phase is important. If your players are having fun and riffing off one another, let them continue and build/write/draw together. Of course, you're the game master so you can direct them when needed or reign in elements that don't belong in the narrative/campaign. Once the map is complete enough, use the randomly generated content and also the drop table lists toward the end of the book that turns the map into a playable game board.

Use the back inside cover and blank end papers for neighboring towns, cities, or locations. Players can use those pages as well, drawing their properties in more detail. Basically, the guts of this book are reserved for the GM.

If it makes sense for you, use the same color or symbol system to mark the map(s) where events occurred in relation to those players/characters. Likewise, use those same colors or symbols to match other pages to unify occurrences visually—this will make it easier to understand and remember the relationships you're building.

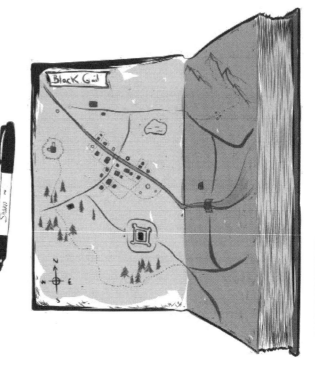

If your characters get stuck, have them roll the random backstory generators to create their map. This creates their backstory and bonds your characters as they add more and more to the map. Use as many of the randomly generated locations/events as you want, but you're definitely not meant to use them all.

As the GM, it might be a good tension driver to choose some scarcities. Maybe the area doesn't have good hunting and protein is scarce. Is it possible that drinking water is hard to find? Let your characters know what is scarce and what is plentiful in the area. If your characters roll a randomly generated description that conflicts with this scarcity, you will have to tweak the description. Again, change and adapt this book to fit your campaign and never feel pigeonholed into compromise unless it adds to your story.

Optional non-linear subplots are just that, mere suggestions. As the GM, you can create whatever makes sense for your party. These suggestions can be used literally or built upon or ignored outright.

D20 Alliances and Conflict

1. Alliance - Choose two characters who are now in-laws. They must decide how and when this happened. Their families get along well—better than most family alliances in the area. Resources are shared between families and family members can learn trades and hobbies from one another. Characters now draw on the map a small and secret dwelling that both families own and use as a common meeting place. Someone is usually there guarding it and tending to the property.

For the Campaign (optional non-linear subplot) - A family member can appear in a scene, maybe kidnapped, maybe turned evil / the two characters hear that the families were attacked while they were away.

2. Conflict - All characters roll initiative. Highest and lowest got into a drunken fist fight one night at the local tavern. No one won the fight, but there's been bad blood for a while over this scuffle. The lowest rolling character lost a tooth. The highest rolling character found a small amount of money on the ground after the fight. Characters draw this tavern on the map where the fight occurred and name it. They're banned from there for one week.

For the Campaign (optional non-linear subplot) - An NPC can bring up the fight and stoke tensions / witnesses of the fight spread rumors and now people are afraid of the two characters / an NPC wants to fight both characters at once to prove they're superior / an NPC is reluctant to help the party because they witnessed the fight.

3. Alliance - Choose two characters that share the same hobby and learn from each other regularly. It also increases a stat related to this hobby when they both share their experiences. Characters must determine what this hobby is, what stat it relates to, and where—on the map—this hobby occurs. Characters now draw the location and/or dwelling on the map.

For the Campaign (optional non-linear subplot) - The party meets an NPC that shares this same hobby / the hobby is outlawed where the characters have traveled / party stumbles on a seller or equivalent who specializes in this hobby / a villain finds this hobby appealing / an NPC that a character likes thinks their hobby is ridiculous.

4. Conflict - All characters roll initiative. Lowest character caught fire in a weird accident. Highest came to their rescue, but somehow made it worse. Characters decide how this happened and where. Characters now draw the location on the map where this happened. Lowest character now has a burn scar. Roll 1D6. GM decides the severity of the scar depending on the roll: 1 being the least scarring, 6 being the worst. Lowest character probably blames the highest character though the fire was originally not the highest player's fault.

For the Campaign (optional non-linear subplot) - Fire can become a source of post-traumatic stress for the character / if the character's scar is noticeable, an NPC can comment on it and even assume it is a weakness.

5. Alliance - All characters roll initiative. Highest two characters found a strange talisman while walking together. They have no idea what it does, but they now share its mysterious power. GM decides what this item does in relation to the campaign. On the map, characters now draw where the talisman was found.

For the Campaign (optional non-linear subplot) - Talisman is magic or cursed and belongs to an NPC that the PCs meet lat-

Location or Event

Name _____

History _____

_____

_____

_____

_____

_____

er / talisman belongs to another NPC that was generated by this book and is priceless to that NPC.

6. Conflict - All characters roll initiative. Lowest two characters are in debt to an herbalist who lives on the edge of the town or city. Both characters accidentally damaged the herbalist's wagon badly enough that they want an ample amount of a scarce resource as payment. GM decides what resource this is. Characters draw on the map where the herbalist lives. If the characters pay this herbalist, they will gain this person's trust and receive discounts on items they sell.

For the Campaign (optional non-linear subplot) - Characters discover a source of this scarce resource on their journey / the source of this scarce resource is a creature who must die to give it up / a party member is allergic to this resource / a creature that the party discovers eats this resource and seeks it out.

7. Alliance - Choose two characters who inherited a small tavern in the center of town. Characters now draw this place on the map and name it. GM decides what kind of revenue this establishment can generate each month if it is maintained properly. Characters can also draw a larger version of this tavern in the back of the book on the back cover / end paper. GM can decide if items can be stored there.

For the Campaign (optional non-linear subplot) - Party hears that the property has been raided and taken over while they are away / a distant relative of the person who passed the property to the characters now claims they own it / the property burns to the ground and the GM can decide why or who did it.

Location or Event

Name _____

History _____

_____

_____

_____

_____

8. Conflict - Choose two characters who witnessed a murder. The murderer got away, but now the characters must decide if they wish to hunt this person down. This must be a secret as the murderer is the son or daughter of a very wealthy person in town. On the map, mark where this murderer lives, name them, and give them stats/traits appropriate to your system.

For the Campaign (optional non-linear subplot) - The wealthy parent hears that there were witnesses to this murder and they have sent an assassin to kill the two characters.

9. Alliance - All characters roll initiative. Highest two characters share a lover who is happy with this threesome arrangement. This common lover tells the characters what is happening in town. GM can decide if this NPC has valuable information. GM names this person and characters now draw where they live on the map.

For the Campaign (optional non-linear subplot) - While the party is away, this person is murdered or kidnapped / while the party is away, this person leaves town mysteriously / this person turns out to be somewhat evil.

10. Conflict - All characters roll initiative. Lowest two characters were attacked by some strange and somewhat large creature at night. It tried to drag the lowest initiative character into the woods (or equivalent), but the higher character saved them. Draw where this creature was last seen. GM decides what this creature is, giving it stats and a motive. If the party decides to hunt this creature, the two characters who first discovered it will find treasure from the eaten corpses in the creature's lair.

For the Campaign (optional non-linear subplot) - There are more of these creatures later in the campaign and they know if the party hunted the first creature / the creature was a lost pet of an NPC that the party meets later / creature is intelligent, but mistook the PCs for someone else who harmed it / creature can become a familiar if charmed.

Location or Event

Name _____

History _____

_____

_____

_____

_____

11. Alliance - Choose two characters who befriend an older person who is somewhat of an outcast in the community. Characters now draw where this person's small dwelling is on the map. Characters swear to protect this person even though locals do not trust them. This person calls the characters sons/daughters and also teaches them something very useful about the native environment—this is up to the GM.

For the Campaign (optional non-linear subplot) - This person is murdered while the party is away / this person is corrupt and plays a role in the campaign / this person dies of natural causes.

12. Conflict - Choose two characters who were gambling one night and they both lost to a person that they suspected was cheating. The lowest character in the initiative followed this cheater out of the tavern and either beat them up or killed them, depending on their alignment or character type. The other character disagreed with this violence, unconvinced the cheater actually cheated. Characters decide if they split the money that the lowest initiative character took from this "cheater".

Location or Event

Name _____

History _____

_____

_____

_____

_____

_____

Characters now draw the tavern on the map. The cheater's friends now wish both player's harm. They hang out at this tavern frequently.

For the Campaign (optional non-linear subplot) - Friends of the "cheating" NPC show up later in the campaign / friends of the "cheating" NPC burn the tavern to the ground / friends of the "cheating" NPC throw a memorial service at the tavern.

13. Alliance - All characters roll initiative. Highest two characters either share a weapon type or a spell type. When they work together, they can have bonuses. **GM** decides what this means according to the systems you are using.

For the Campaign (optional non-linear subplot) - Whatever this weapon type or spell type is, it is taboo or illegal to use / another player distrusts or is weak to this weapon or magic / a villain specializes in this weapon or magic as well.

14. Conflict - All characters roll initiative. Lowest two characters sometimes share the same dream. They interpret this as a vision, but the **GM** must decide what it means. Is it a God? Is it just paranoia? Is it a ghost? **GM** draws a place on the map where both characters are drawn to—a place where they've both dreamt about. This dream will reoccur throughout the campaign.

For the Campaign (optional non-linear subplot) - These dreams have a lasting affect on the players, making them paranoid or stressed / players can warp back to that place in the town/city where the dream occurs / an **NPC** is trying to communicate with them through this dream.

15. Alliance - All characters roll initiative. Highest two characters are very skilled at hunting a medium-sized native beast that stalks the surrounding area. Locals revere the characters for their bravery. An armorer makes light armor out of the skins and gave the characters a complimentary pair of armor sets. **GM** assigns stats to armor. Players now draw where this armorer's shop is on the map.

Location or Event

Name _____

History _____

_____

_____

_____

_____

_____

For the Campaign (optional non-linear subplot) - A larger creature loves the taste of the medium-sized beast and will sniff out anyone who is wearing this armor / this armor gives players a bonus to certain attacks, but is weak to other elemental attacks / an **NPC** is horrified that anyone would wear the hide of this beast / the armor attracts gnats and mites or other parasites that are found outside the town/city.

16. Conflict - Choose two characters who both need the same scarce resource for different reasons. Characters decide what this is and how it pertains to their character's needs. It must be something they care deeply about. On the map, **GM** draws where this resource can be obtained. Lowest initiative character has half as much as the other player.

For the Campaign (optional non-linear subplot) - Party finds a cache of this resource on their journey / an **NPC** also needs this resource / this resource is poisonous to some locals or creatures.

17. Alliance - All characters roll initiative. Highest two characters are favored by the local authorities for their skills. They are offered occasional side work although the nature of these jobs might be questionable. **GM** decides what this means. **GM** now draws two locations where the local authorities meet, one public and one secret location (only known by the party).

Location or Event

Name

History

For the Campaign (optional non-linear subplot) - These side jobs are all secretly aimed at harming a powerful NPC / side jobs reward players with increasing (compounding) experience / there is a rival party also working these side jobs and they are willing to kill.

18. Conflict - All characters roll initiative. Lowest two characters find out that a migration of destitute people have entered the area. The local authorities have captured them, separated the children from the parents, and housed them in makeshift "shelters" which are more like jails. Players now draw these shelters on the map: one for the adults and one for the children. Both characters who rolled have been asked to join a party to break out the migrants and release them, agreeing the migrants will leave the area right away. GM decides the outcome and repercussions of this attempted breakout.

For the Campaign (optional non-linear subplot) - Freed people later come to the party's aid, authorities find out that the party helped free the people and send mercenaries after the party / freed people are later found dead.

19. Alliance - Choose two characters who saved a family as their house burned to the ground. Two of their children were trapped on the second floor. Characters describe how this happened and draw the location of the fire and also the location of the family's new home. GM must create names and traits for this family of NPCs. These two characters will always have a place to stay as the family is forever grateful.

For the Campaign (optional non-linear subplot) - An NPC confesses to burning the family's house / one of the children runs away and finds the party.

Conflict - All characters roll initiative. Lowest two characters were drunk one night and lost a valuable object down a well. Players now draw this well on the map. GM decides what the object was and if the PCs can retrieve it. The well could lead to something even more valuable.

For the Campaign (optional non-linear subplot) - The well leads to a secret cave / the item is never found in the well, but somewhere during the campaign, it is mysteriously found.

D20 A River Runs, Joins, and Divides

1. A large river runs through town, providing vital resources and recreation when times are good. Characters draw this river on the map including a small bridge. Choose two characters who stash things behind a loose stone in the bridge. GM decides what is hidden there. No other characters know what is there unless these two characters tell them.

For the Campaign (optional non-linear subplot) - The items are stolen and can only be found if the players wait by the bridge after stashing more items there to see who took the first items / for some mysterious reason, other items are found in this location when the players return / this location has an emotional connection for these two players.

2. A river lies at the edge of town where it forks south into two smaller rivers. Characters draw this river on the map. Choose two characters who witnessed a young boy drown there and mark where it happened with a symbol. Now the characters must draw a nearby house—small and modest—where the family of the dead young boy lives. GM decides what the family is like, but there must be a mother, father, brother, and sister.

For the Campaign (optional non-linear subplot) - One of the children blames one of the players for the drowning although it makes no sense / a strange creature caused the drowning who the party encounter later in the campaign / another child drowns from the same family in the same river, causing alarm in the community / the parents blame the characters for not saving the young boy from drowning.

3. There is a river that runs along the east side of town. Characters draw this river on the map. One two-lane bridge is the only crossing for miles. It's a very sturdy stone bridge that has stood for longer than

most can remember. At night, something odd happens. The water under the center of the bridge slows while the water around it flows normally. It's as if there is an invisible oval blocking the current. In the morning, the water returns to normal. Choose two characters who have witnessed this. **GM** will decide what this phenomenon is.

For the Campaign (optional non-linear subplot) - An NPC's magic is affecting the flow of the water in the area, but this NPC doesn't realize it / jumping into the river while this is happening teleports players / looking into this weird occurrence shows visions of the future (campaign).

4. A large river runs along the edge of town where a watermill sits, churning day and night. Characters draw this river and watermill which has a small house attached to it. Choose one char-

Map Assets

copy, cut, and paste
then add to and color if you wish

acter who has befriended the owner of the mill. The owner can provide scarcities and goods. GM decides what the scarcities are and who this owner is. Another player, of the GM's choice, does not trust this mill owner for a reason that the GM will create.

For the Campaign (optional non-linear subplot) - Something has stopped the flow of the water to the mill which is jeopardizing this friend's livelihood / the friend is a relation of someone who shows up later in the campaign / the friend has a monopoly on certain resources and it negatively affects NPCs that the party cares about.

5. There is a modest size river that flows along the edge of town. Characters draw this river on the map. It overflows every few years when there is a heavy downpour. Choose one character who was caught in a recent flood, but saved by a local woman who lives downstream. The character nearly died. Draw this woman's small shack. The character is in debt to this woman. The woman is also related to another player—the GM decides how they are related.

For the Campaign (optional non-linear subplot) - Party finds out this woman was murdered or kidnapped while they are off adventuring / to repay the debt, this woman wants the player to do something somewhat difficult / this woman can predict the future.

6. There is a strange river that cuts through the area a little ways from town. Characters draw this river and the dense forest around it. Two characters of the GM's choice hike through this area to fish in this remote river, sometimes catching large fish that are valuable at the local market. Sometimes the characters camp half way between the river and town. On those nights, they hear odd bark/croaking from the direction of the shore. GM decides what this bark/croaking is and if it means anything.

For the Campaign (optional non-linear subplot) - Cursed Wolf/Frog Men, either hostile or friendly populate the area / a pack of children enjoy pranking locals and dress in weird Frog Men costumes made from local materials / witches populate the area and collect large bullfrogs at night.

7. There is a wide river close to town where boats often pass by. Characters draw this river on the map. Two characters recently witnessed a flaming boat crash into shore, its passengers all overboard and missing. In the boat were items of the GM's choosing. A day later, a man entered town, his arms badly burnt. He is penniless and now sleeps under a large tree in a nearby forest. Characters draw the tree on the map. If characters befriend this man, GM chooses who he is and what it means to possibly get some of the found possessions back.

For the Campaign (optional non-linear subplot) - This man is related to other people in the campaign / this man will become a friend and ally in battle if needed although he is suffering from post-traumatic stress from the accident / this man caused the fire on the boat and only tells the party later once they have earned his trust.

8. There is a thin river that flows through town. An herbalist lives in a modest house along the shore. Characters draw both the river and the house on the map. The herbalist is attracted to one of the characters and offers them discounts on items. GM decides what character this is and what the herbalist is like. Another character does not trust this herbalist and will have nothing to do with any item or elixir or whatever they gave the party. The herbalist also allows the party to rest at this house when they wish.

For the Campaign (optional non-linear subplot) - The herbalist is related to another NPC who was generated by this book / the herbalist understands the area well and can answer mysteries generated by this book / the character that distrusts this herbalist has keen intuition because the herbalist is a shapeshifter and appears later in the campaign.

9. A river separates two very different sections of town. A large bridge connects the two areas. Characters draw this river and the bridge. GM decides what distinguishes the two sides. One

character of the GM's choosing is either from one area or prefers it for some reason. Another character of the GM's choosing owns property in the other area. That character now draws the property, which is modest. Name these two areas of town.

For the Campaign (optional non-linear subplot) - One of the characters is friendly with a gang from one side of town / a trade war is happening between the two sides of town / a secret tunnel underneath the river connects buildings that are on either side / an NPC from the campaign is from one side of town and is heavily invested in it.

10. A large river provides essential resources for the town. It flows straight through town though a dam to the north keeps it from overflowing. Characters draw this river and dam on the map. One night, a player's relative led a party of raiders to the dam and damaged it, flooding houses along the shore that the raiders pillaged. People were murdered and many valuable items were taken. Another character of the GM's choice had a relative murdered by these raiders.

For the Campaign (optional non-linear subplot) - These raiders were hired by an NPC that shows up later in the campaign / the raider's stash is discovered and a player recognizes items that once belonged to their murdered relatives / players have to oversee the reconstruction of the dam as more raiders attack.

11. At a tavern one night, a stranger spoke about a sunken boat at the bottom of the town's river. A character of the GM's choice overheard this and what might have been on board when the boat sank. Characters draw the river, but only one character knows the location of the boat (which they can draw or keep secret). GM decides what was on this boat when it sank. GM also decides if one character is a poor swimmer.

For the Campaign (optional non-linear subplot) - Party meets the original owner of the boat / party finds out who sunk the boat and why.

12. Something died upstream in the large river that cuts through town.

Characters draw this river on the map and also the location of the carcass. Not knowing the river was polluted, townspeople have been consuming the water and getting violently ill. GM decides what died in the water. GM chooses a character who has taken ill and is close to death. GM chooses a character who nursed this sick character back to health. Sick character is now in the healer character's debt.

For the Campaign (optional non-linear subplot) - Someone poisoned and killed this creature and intentionally poisoned the river / these creatures are relatively harmless and live where the party is traveling, but someone or something removed it from its native habitat.

13. A fishing community lives along the shore of a large river. Characters draw this river anywhere on the map. Recently, the community was attacked and two characters of the GM's choice came to their rescue. Thankful, the community built a somewhat life-like driftwood sculpture in honor of the two characters and regularly give them fish in thanks. The people or creatures who attacked the community should be named and described by the GM.

For the Campaign (optional non-linear subplot) - These people or creatures were made to attack the fishing community by an NPC the party encounters later / fishing community creates an effective fighting force against these attackers and GM names the group.

14. Recently, a noble has started building a dam north of the river that flows through town. Characters draw this river and the partly-constructed dam. The townspeople are panicked as they rely on the water for drinking and trading. GM chooses a character who is loyal to the noble for a personal reason. GM also chooses a character who has family that relies heavily on the river for trading. Characters can choose what to do about this conflict.

For the Campaign (optional non-linear subplot) - Nobleman will offer party wealth to align with him / nobleman appears later in the campaign either captured or empowered / nobleman closes dam while party is away adventuring, causing havoc among the community.

15. Choose a character who fell in the river that cuts through town. Characters draw this river on the map and the location in which the character fell in. GM chooses what item they lost in the water. Characters roll initiative. Highest character that is not the character that fell in the river went back to this location and searched for hours until they recovered the lost item. This character can give the item back if they wish.

For the Campaign (optional non-linear subplot) - This item is now cursed by something that lives in the river and the curse can be lifted by someone the party meets later in the campaign / the item is now marked by a being and the item acts as a beacon.

16. There is a river along the edge of town that is a thoroughfare for boats. Characters draw this river on the map. Recently, raiders sailed downriver and plundered a caravan of trading boats before they reached town. Many of the robbed merchants docked here and now meander through town in a state of depression. Many of them are staying for free in a shack on the other side of town. Characters draw the shack. Choose a character that knows the secret location of the raiders. That character draws the location. It is rumored that these raiders have a stash of a scarcity (chosen by the GM).

For the Campaign (optional non-linear subplot) - Raiders are part of a larger group that the party will eventually encounter / raiders have amassed a treasure, but the party will need help defeating them.

17. A friend of two characters (chosen by the GM) drowned in the river. Characters draw this river on the map and the location where the friend drowned. This friend was very popular in town. About a dozen townspeople built a makeshift memorial to the friend close to the town tavern. Characters draw a tavern if there isn't a prominent one already. GM names this dead friend. The dead friend will visit these two player's dreams every now and then.

For the Campaign (optional non-linear subplot) - Someone drowned the friend on purpose and the party finds out who later in the campaign / friend's brother or sister or both are encountered in the campaign and they are looking for the person who drowned their sibling / friend's ghost appears sometimes—voiceless and water-filled.

18. Choose two characters who own a small boat that they dock along a river that runs through town. Characters draw both the river and the small boat on the map. It's been stolen by someone who the GM creates. GM can decide where the boat is now and if the characters will ever recover it. GM also decides if the characters lost any loot that happened to be inside the boat.

For the Campaign (optional non-linear subplot) - Characters encounter the NPC(s) who took their boat later in the campaign as well as recover any lost items / a non-threatening NPC needed the boat for a nobel cause.

19. A large river runs through town. Characters draw this river on the map. GM choses two characters who saw a small boat sink along the water's edge one night. The person on the boat was murdered—their body floating along the shore. GM decides what treasure and cursed items were on the boat, assuming that the characters searched the wreckage. Both characters roll initiative. Lowest character almost drowned trying to scavenge loot from the wreckage. The other character saved them from drowning.

For the Campaign (optional non-linear subplot) - Characters encounter the murder later in the campaign / any items taken from the wreckage are later recognized by someone and mistakes the PCs as murderers.

20. There is a modest size river that flows along the outskirts of town. Characters draw this river on the map. GM chooses two characters who are great swimmers. These two characters used to race each other, swimming back and forth from shore to shore. GM can make characters roll to see how many races each won and crown one character the winner. There is also a townsperson (NPC) who both characters wanted to win the affection of. This person admires strength.

GM decides which swimming rivalry plays into this admiration. GM creates this townsperson and draws where they live on the map.

For the Campaign (optional non-linear subplot) - NPC that admires the strongest swimmer falls in love with them and is abducted one night / NPC begins to fall in love with a different PC after admiring the strongest swimmer.

D12 Education

1. Choose two characters who were educated together in a local trade. GM decides what makes sense for these two. It cannot be something that would dramatically alter the player's character, but it should be something that is meaningful to both players. If it makes sense, draw the location on the map where the two characters were educated and name the mentor who works/lives there. Roll a 50/50 chance die to see if this mentor is still alive. Characters are allowed to have one artifact from this training and they share it.

For the Campaign (optional non-linear subplot) - This trade can come in handy during the campaign / if mentor is alive, they are abducted or are turned evil and appear later in the campaign.

2. Choose two characters who were educated together in a regionally specific and somewhat trivial magic. Have the characters roll initia-

tive and make the highest character better at this magic than the other player. If it makes sense, draw the location on the map where the two characters were educated and name the mentor who works/lives there. Roll a 50/50 chance die to see if this mentor is still alive. Characters are allowed to have one artifact from this training and they share it.

For the Campaign (optional non-linear subplot) - This magic might be stronger where the party is traveling / if mentor is alive, they were abducted / the magic has odd side effects.

3. Choose three characters who were educated together in a specialized combat. Have the characters roll initiative and make the highest character better at this combat than the other players. The lowest rolled character dropped out of training and isn't good at all. This training might make sense if it's grappling or some sort of unarmed fighting style. Characters now draw the location on the map where the two characters were educated and the GM names the mentor who works/lives there. Roll a 50/50 chance die to see if this mentor is still alive. Characters are allowed to have one artifact from this training and they share it.

For the Campaign (optional non-linear subplot) - Certain enemies are weak to this combat / if the mentor is alive, they were abducted and are now forced to train evil NPCs / most locals very much admire anyone who is well trained in this combat style.

4. Choose two characters who shared the same lover who is well-known and admired. Have both characters roll initiative. The highest rolled player's relationship with this person is a secret while the lowest rolled player's relationship with them is not a secret—the whole town knows. Name this NPC and have the lowest rolled character draw where they live on the map. Both characters must give up 1/10th of their money as they've already spent it on gifts for this NPC.

For the Campaign (optional non-linear subplot) - NPC is abducted / NPC is corrupted and encountered later in the campaign / NPC moves away without explanation / a villain is in love with the NPC.

5. Choose two characters who were educated together in something nautical related: sailing, ship building, or even diving. Have the characters roll initiative and make the highest character better at this craft than the other character. If it makes sense, draw the location on the map where the two characters were educated and name the mentor who works/lives there. Roll a 50/50 chance die to see if this mentor is still alive. Characters are allowed to have one artifact from this training and they share it.

For the Campaign (optional non-linear subplot) - This craft comes in handy during the campaign / mentor is abducted if they are still alive / if mentor is dead, a younger relative arrives and they demand to be trained in the craft so they can pass it on to their children.

6. Choose two characters who were educated together in drawing and painting. Have the characters roll initiative and make the highest character better at this craft than the other player. If it makes sense, draw the location on the map where the two characters were educated and name the mentor who works/lives there. Roll a 50/50 chance die to see if this mentor is still alive. Name two NPCs who were students of the mentor. One of the characters had a relationship with one of the students. GM decides what this means. Characters decide if they kept any artwork from their lessons and where it is stored.

For the Campaign (optional non-linear subplot) - Paintings and drawings may be valuable and used as currency / most talented PC has a patron who collects their work / most talented PC has an admirer who will sit for portraits any time the PC wants / a villain is an art collector.

7. Choose two characters who were educated in dance. They can now assist each other in modest acrobatic maneuvers. Have both characters roll initiative making the lowest character victim to a fall: they broke their ankle during training. This was a while ago so there is no lasting pain, but arthritis might be an issue at some point. If it makes sense, draw the location on the map where the two characters were

educated and name the mentor who works/lives there. Roll a 50/50 chance die to see if this instructor is still alive. Characters are allowed to have one artifact from this training and they share it. GM decides if there is a romantic relationship between the dance instructor and one of the players.

For the Campaign (optional non-linear subplot) - If the mentor is alive, they have been abducted / certain enemies are weak to acrobatic attacks / some NPCs can be charmed with dance / there's a location in town where performances are hosted and dance is admired by many.

8. Choose two characters who were educated in carpentry. They built a small dwelling together and they both own it, but rent it to a friend for very little money. Have them draw the dwelling on the map and name the friend. Now have them draw a half-finished fence. Now have them draw a smashed cart in the back of the dwelling. Now have them draw a slaughtered dog that's hung in a nearby tree. Now have them draw a hole in the roof of the dwelling. The friend has been killed by raiders and no one knows where they went.

For the Campaign (optional non-linear subplot) - Raiders are encountered later in the campaign and one of them has possessions of the dead friend / carpentry comes in handy during the campaign / side jobs are available for carpenters in town.

9. Choose two characters who were educated in masonry. Have the characters draw a modest stone wall they built for a friend as well as the house it surrounds on the map. Characters might now

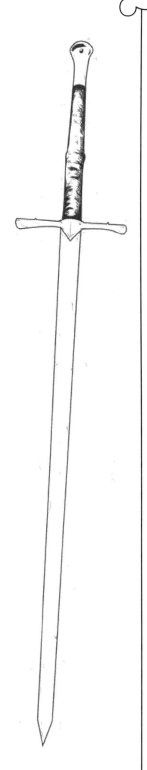

have an acute sense of geology and their natural environment. If it makes sense, draw the location on the map where the two characters were educated and name the mentor who works/lives there. Roll a 50/50 chance die to see if this mentor is still alive. Characters are allowed to have one artifact from this training and they share it.

For the Campaign (optional non-linear subplot) - Masonry might be the lowliest trade of the land / there's jobs to be had for masons, maybe one that pays well and leads to more plot: the person who commissioned the work is up to something nefarious or building what they are asked is in opposition to an NPC who was already created by this book or has a key role in the campaign.

10. Choose two characters who were educated in sleight of hand as well as "magic." This is very elementary trickery, but it can come in handy when communicating with lesser or unintelligent beings. Children in the town/city the characters live in love to see this weird stuff and even call the characters nicknames (GM decides what they are). If it makes sense, draw the location on the map where the two characters were educated and name the mentor who works/lives there. Roll a 50/50 chance die to see if this mentor is still alive. Characters are allowed to have one artifact from this training and they share it.

For the Campaign (optional non-linear subplot) - Mentor is mistaken for a witch or evil wizard and is arrested / some NPCs can be tricked with this magic / this magic is outlawed in certain lands.

11. Choose two characters who were trained in hunting a local animal of which the GM creates. Have both characters roll initiative making the higher character better at hunting. This can factor into their character skills, especially when engaging NPCs that have similar features as the local animal. If it makes sense, draw the location on the map where the two characters were educated and name the mentor who works/lives there. Roll a 50/50 chance die to see if this mentor is still alive. Characters are allowed to have one artifact from this training and they share it.

For the Campaign (optional non-linear subplot) - Hides of this animal are valuable / there is a hunting expedition about to begin or is encountered later in the campaign / there is an annual hunting festival for tracking down these creatures / a local weapon smith specializes in creating items specifically to hunt these creatures / a villain adores these creatures and has many as familiars.

12. Choose two characters who apprenticed as blacksmiths, but never finished their training. Have both characters roll initiative making the higher character a better smith. This can factor into their character skills. Characters now draw the location on the map where the two characters were educated and name the mentor who lived there but is now dead. They were murdered in the streets by unknown assailants. Characters are allowed to have one artifact from this training and they share it.

For the Campaign (optional non-linear subplot) - Unknown assailants can be tracked down with a little investigative work / blacksmithing comes in handy during the campaign.

D6 Walls Both Big and Small

1. There's a fortified wall that surrounds all of the town/city, a portion of which is damaged from age. Characters draw this wall on the map. GM chooses two characters that helped rebuild the damaged portion of the wall. Townspeople in nearby houses appreciate the hard work because bandits and/or creatures have been known to enter through that weak point. GM draws the nearby houses and names any important characters

that live there, deciding what modest gifts the townspeople gave the two characters as a thank you. Characters also befriended one NPC more than the rest. GM decides who this is after both characters roll initiative. Highest rolling character becomes good friends with this appreciative NPC who may have helpful resources and/or advice.

For the Campaign (optional non-linear subplot) - After all that work, raiders damage the wall again and harm the people nearby / something lives underneath the wall and is caving it in / one of the locals damaged the wall in the first place and will do it again for nefarious reasons.

2. There's an old stone wall that zigzags outside town, much of which is broken or buried in overgrown trees. Characters draw this partial wall on the map. GM chooses two characters that fought a roving band of raiders at the furthest point along the wall away from town. The two characters made quick work of these raiders and the GM should let them decide how they dealt with them. Both characters roll initiative. The highest rolled character kept a trophy or trophies from one of the raiders. GM decides what it is. This trophy might be too heavy for two people to transport.

For the Campaign (optional non-linear subplot) - The NPCs that the characters dispatched are part of a larger gang / the roving band was looking for something along the zigzagging wall / the same style of zigzagging wall reappears later in the campaign.

3. A squat stone wall circles a small graveyard. Characters draw this walled graveyard on the map. GM chooses two characters that buried a good friend there recently. They put their money together to create a proper headstone as this friend had no family to construct a proper grave. Nearby, the dead friend's tiny home sits. Characters draw this home as well. They now own this little piece of property. If they search, there is a secret cellar where the friend practiced black magic. GM can decide what is down there: loot or more secrets.

For the Campaign (optional non-linear subplot) - The friend was secretly part of a cult that practices powerful magic / the friend had enemies that the party encounters later in the campaign / someone or something desecrated the grave and took the dead friend's body / dead friend is reanimated and encountered later in the campaign.

4. Someone or something has built a thick waist-high wall made of thickets and vines in the forest. There is no gate. It winds around a pond. Characters draw this strange wall and pond on the map. GM chooses two characters who use this pond as a swimming area, but they sense something strange about the place. Locals think the pond has restorative powers and some people even travel from far away to wade in the waters. GM decides what it is. GM can make characters roll for initiative to see which is positively or negatively affected by the place.

For the Campaign (optional non-linear subplot) - Something lives deep inside the pond / someone in the area is responsible for the pond's somewhat restorative powers / the pond begins to attract unsavory people and beings / a person wants to bottle the water and sell it.

5. There's a large wall that runs through town that divides the well-off and poorer classes. Choose two players, one being from one side and one being from the other. GM can make them roll for this if they wish. These two characters are in the same party despite their different upbringings because the poorer character caught a kid as they fell from the top of the wall—the kid being from the wealthy side, the character catching from the poorer side. The kid would have been crippled or killed otherwise so the poorer character is now a local hero. Characters draw this wall on the map and also the spot where the poorer character caught the kid. GM can decide what this means to their families, if they have families. Have the characters explain more about how this dynamic feeds into their relationship. GM names the kid who can also have a larger role in the campaign.

For the Campaign (optional non-linear subplot) - The kid comes from a very wealthy family who takes care of the character who caught him / the kid grows to be influential despite their young age / the kid becomes evil / the kid is something of a loose cannon and gets into trouble.

Drop Slide Table Instructions

DROP

Choose two characters, one will be one on the
left side (this side) and one will be on the right side
(the other page).

Hold the book in the V shape in one hand so you can
shake and drop 3D6 on the circle and have them slide down
the spine and stack on the tip of your thumb.

The Drop Slide Table makes two characters
compete for the better number on the same die.
This way there are two "tops" to each die roll.
Use these tables when two characters are
affected by the same occurrence and you want to
create tension.

SLIDE

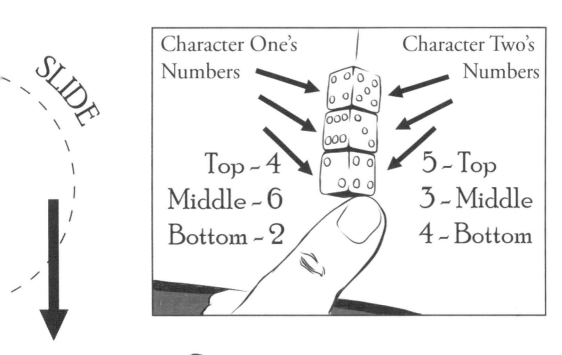

Character One's Numbers   Character Two's Numbers

Top ~ 4   5 ~ Top
Middle ~ 6   3 ~ Middle
Bottom ~ 2   4 ~ Bottom

TEMPORARY MAGIC BUFF OR BLESSING FOR 2 CHARACTERS

DROP

GM decides duration of effect

Top D6

1. All food tastes absolutely delicious.
2. Acute hearing.
3. See in dark.
4. Advantage on most cerebral tasks.
5. Head-butting enemies causes near critical damage.
6. Substantially increased intelligence and charisma.

Middle D6

1. Remarkably lovely, soft hands.
2. One thumbnail is dagger-sharp and caused poison.
3. One punch equals the attack of a spiked mace.
4. Advantage on all strength abilities.
5. Able to wield 2 two-handed weapons.
6. Substantially increased defense.

Bottom D6

1. Adorable feet, enviably so.
2. Increased speed and libido.
3. Kicking can easily disarm enemies.
4. Skilled at climbing and descending on enemies.
5. Able to walk over dangerous surfaces.
6. Substantially increased agility and speed.

MULTIPLE DAMAGE POINTS
FOR 2 CHARACTERS

SLIDE

GM decides severity of damage

Top D6

1. Slight scar on face.
2. Noticeable scar on face.
3. Missing tooth.
4. Broken and now somewhat crooked nose.
5. Ear torn off.
6. Missing eye.

Middle D6

1. Scar on arm and broken finger.
2. Large scar on chest and broken hand.
3. Broken rib compromising 1 stat.
4. Damaged lungs compromising 2 stats.
5. Chest pain and heart weakened compromising 3 stats.
6. Organ failure with lasting affects compromising 3 stats.

Bottom D6

1. Broken toe and compromised mobility.
2. Smashed shin and compromised mobility.
3. Broken foot and decreased mobility.
4. Severely cut thigh and bleeding heavily.
5. Broken leg and decreased mobility.
6. Two broken legs and severely decreased mobility.

LOOT DROP FROM LARGE OR MID-LEVEL NPC FOR 2 CHARACTERS

DROP

GM decides magic bonuses and restrictions (if any)

Top D6

1. Eye patch that smells horrible.
2. Gold earrings that belong to an NPC, very valuable.
3. Low-level helmet that turns your head invisible.
4. High-pitched whistle that causes area damage.
5. Fire-resistant cloak, could be magic. Also 1D20 gold.
6. Mid to high level helmet, could be magic.

Middle D6

1. Shirt with several human fingers in pocket.
2. Low level mace, cracked, yet darkly magical.
3. Crossbow with eight bolts. Also 1D20 gold.
4. Mid level magic staff once owned by an NPC.
5. Plate armor, maybe magic, wearable by anyone.
6. Mid to high level arming sword, magic. Leaf blade.

Bottom D6

1. Rotting leather shoes that attract animals.
2. Mid level chainmail kilt.
3. Plate armor for waist, legs, and feet. Also 1D20 gold.
4. Boots that do heavy kicking/stomping damage.
5. Magical pants that turn you invisible for a limited time.
6. Magical leather boots that increase all physical stats. One boot has a spur that can also cause damage.

MULTIPLE MAGIC CHARMS/FAMILIARS
FOR 2 CHARACTERS

SLIDE

GM clarifies details and scales stats appropriately

Top D6

1. Handkerchief, "alive" like a familiar though easily burned.
2. Silver necklace that heals 1D4 HP per day.
3. Charming skullcap that is as strong as a mid level helmet.
4. Cute vampire bat, sleeps on your shoulder, mid level stats, farts.
5. Makeup case, makeup transforms your face into any other face.
6. Black mask with horns. Lightning-like spell blast from mouth.

Middle D6

1. Thin, blood stained shirt that repels some common beasts.
2. Leather bracer with a poisonous, friendly worm living inside it.
3. Belt with many compartments, filled with healing potions.
4. Large, four-eyed snake with mid level stats. Speaks.
5. Ring that imbues weapons with fire damage for limited time.
6. Light chainmail with the strength of plate mail, fire resistant.

Bottom D6

1. Toe ring. Ugly. Very valuable. Alive. Whispers at night.
2. Comfortable shoes that increase 1 stat for a while.
3. Anklet that magically grows into a whip with mid level damage.
4. A bear that loves to be rode... actually requires it unless sleeping.
5. Male or female sprite, very small, mid level stats, very attractive.
6. Reptile or dragon, small, mid level stats, immune to most
   magical attacks. Wears valuable silver collar.

MUTATIONS AND EFFECTS
FOR 2 CHARACTERS

DROP

GM decides details and duration of effect

Top D6

1. Hair grows 1 foot per hour.
2. Boil on cheek that slowly seeps a useful toxin.
3. Nose leaks a neon green, low level healing elixir.
4. Fangs, poisonous, and blacked out pupils.
5. Horns that scare religious and some intelligent NPCs.
6. Third eye, yellow pupil, blasts a stream of energy equal to mid level damage.

Middle D6

1. Wiggly skin tag under armpit that speaks/sings.
2. Veins burst from palms like thin tentacles. Range, low damage.
3. Talon-like fingernails with low to mid level damage + bleed.
4. Small bird-like wings that allow you to hover 2 feet.
5. Scales grow over chest, arms, legs equal to mid level armor.
6. Dagger-like onyx blades grow from knuckles. Painful. Mid level damage.

Bottom D6

1. Toenails fall off, but, if eaten, they have mid level healing affect.
2. Very large feet. Loud. Mid level stomping damage.
3. A long, whip-like tail and satyr legs.
4. Reptile legs that are heavily armored, can deal mid level damage.
5. Strong amphibian legs allow you to swim, jump, and more.
6. Centaur. You are now a centaur.

MADNESS, TRAUMA , AND BLIGHT
FOR 2 CHARACTERS

SLIDE

GM decides severity of armor class and damage

Top D6

1. Annoyed, all the time, about small things.
2. Kleptomaniac. You steal party items while PCs sleep.
3. You have a powerful crush on a party member or enemy.
4. The next familiar to join the party disgusts you.
5. You sympathize with a fascist or authoritarian regime.
6. Madness and toxic paranoia against the party.

Middle D6

1. Heartbroken enough to distract you during important events.
2. A spirit / ghost of a death NPC visits you at night.
3. Arthritis. Your hands fail you at the worst times.
4. Asthma that is severe enough to compromise dexterity.
5. Your liver is weak and you cannot consume much alcohol.
6. Your heart is weakened by some magic curse. It compromises all of your physical stats.

Bottom D6

1. Inflammation. Sore feet and ankles slow you down.
2. Restless legs. They keep you awake and reduce your healing.
3. Clumsy all of a sudden. You tend to trip or fumble.
4. You feel the need to dance out of nowhere once a day.
5. For some unknown reason, you stomp loudly quite often.
6. Overwhelmed. You run from tough battles.

6. Choose a character whose family is building a large wall around their large home. Player now draws this wall and home on the map. Choose another character whose relatives are being paid a very low salary to construct this wall. One of the family members was also hurt badly while working and cannot walk well enough to work.

For the Campaign (optional non-linear subplot) - The family fires all the workers and hires other people because the wall is taking too long / the family has a secret to hide and is walling in their home to keep their secret / the family is simply paranoid and scared of outsiders.

D10 Nearby Locations

1. Choose two characters who travel a short distance to a neighboring settlement to let loose. GM describes what this settlement is like while the two characters draw the location in the back of the book on no more than half a page and later on the larger map to locate it. This settlement is ideally makeshift and populated by unsavory people, bandits, and road agents. There can be some neutral NPCs there—people or beings that trade with the less friendly population.

For the Campaign (optional non-linear subplot) - This settlement is destroyed by an NPC from the campaign / some of the population of the party's current town/city dislike this settlement / raiders have completely taken over this settlement and are recruiting others from neighboring towns / the road to the settlement is blocked by road agents who the PCs have to encounter / an NPC generated by this book moves to the settlement against their family's or friend's wishes.

2. Choose two characters who know of an old, destroyed castle in a densely wooded area not far from the town/city. Characters now draw this castle on the larger map and also in the back of the book, taking up no more than half a page. Camping there one night, the characters were attacked and one of them was badly injured. Winning the fight was worth it though—the attackers carried valuable items.

This destroyed castle can become the party's fort, but it will take some repairs (and probably money/labor) to return it to a livable dwelling.

For the Campaign (optional non-linear subplot) - The castle was destroyed during a war that left a lasting impression on the locals / something is slumbering underneath this location / a prominent battle occurs here later in the campaign / a large creature finds this castle a perfect place to call home.

3. Choose two characters who explored the surrounding area and found a hill where a colony of magic users live. These two characters now draw this location on the map and then a larger version of the colony in the back of the book taking up no more than half a page. During this exploration of the area, these two characters saved a magic user from a band of thieves. The magic user is in the characters' debt and invites them to the colony—giving the PCs a safe place to stay anytime they need it. The colony is suspicious of outsiders, but welcomes the PCs (for the most part).

For the Campaign (optional non-linear subplot) - The magic user can train the PCs in basic magic / this colony is attacked later in the campaign / the magic user knows something negative about a location that was already created by this book.

4. Choose two characters who know the surrounding forest well. They have laid traps and stashed provisions and extra weapons in secret places. Have the characters draw this forest on the

map and then also a larger version of the forest in the back of the book taking up no more than a half a page. They will have to decide where traps are laid and where provisions and shelter is.

For the Campaign (optional non-linear subplot) - Enemies can be lured to the forest where the party will have an advantage / PCs don't know that children have been playing in the forest and one of them stumbled into a trap, killing the kid / raiders will use this forest as a regrouping point.

5. Choose two characters who own a herd of animals nearby. This area is fenced and has a small dwelling on it. Characters now draw this on the map and also a larger version in the back of the book taking up no more than half a page. These animals and the land can be sold as well.

For the Campaign (optional non-linear subplot) - Bandits attempt to steal the herd / a magic NPC turns the herd into violent creatures / disease kills 1D10 % of the herd and the disease spreads to a child in the area.

6. Choose two characters who attend the same church outside of town/city. There are many NPCs that are part of this community and they respect these two characters greatly, but urge them to choose non-violence whenever they can. Characters now draw the church on

the map, but also a larger version in the back of the book on no more than half a page. GM names the church and can create the NPCs that worship there. PCs can volunteer to escort NPCs from town to the church as there are sometimes bandits along the route.

For the Campaign (optional non-linear subplot) - A villain burns the church to the ground during a service, killing many / priest of the congregation is secretly a villain / the congregation is suspicious of something that was generated earlier (a location or a NPC).

7. Choose two characters who are friendly with an encampment of unsavory mercenaries not far from town/city. Have the characters draw this encampment on the map as well as a larger version in the back of the book, but not larger than half a page. GM can name this gang or encampment, but also align their allegiance with an existing NPC or a new one. GM can dictate the size of the group, what their interests and motivations are, and if they are interested in another location that has already been created on the map. It might take some effort for the PC to become a trusted ally of these mercenaries.

For the Campaign (optional non-linear subplot) - Unsavory gang's allegiance is bought by a villain that is encountered later in the campaign / an existing NPC in town/city starts an initiative to drive the gang away / gang turns out to be responsible for something negative that already happened during the creation of the map.

8. Choose two characters who killed a giant beast together not long ago. The corpse was so large that they had to leave it. Unfortunately, the rotting stench attracted smaller creatures to the location. Characters now draw this rotted corpse on the map as well as a larger version in the back of the book on no more than half a page. There's a very small village close by that is now threatened by the smaller creatures, many of which have burrowed or nested around the corpse. Taking down this creature might have yielded experience for the characters as well as resources. It way have opened up another portion of the map that the creature was guarding.

For the Campaign (optional non-linear subplot) - The smaller creatures are flourishing and are threatening more locations—the two characters are blamed by locals for this terrible scourge / hunters have moved in and are now creating a small local economy around killing these small creatures, but the hunters are also savage and territorial.

9. Choose two characters who were walking together one day and found an abandoned infant. Characters now draw where they found this infant on the map. This infant will be related to an NPC that was created using this book, decided by the GM. If the infant is safely returned, the NPC will give the PCs a small dwelling outside of the town/city. It can be a place to rest. Characters can draw this location on the map once they are gifted it.

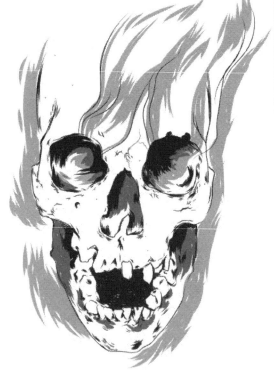

For the Campaign (optional non-linear subplot) - Infant turns out to belong to someone else in the campaign and they blame the PCs for handing it over to the wrong person / infant wasn't really the infant—it is a shapeshifter that murders the NPC and disappears into the night / infant is carrying an infectious disease.

10. Choose two characters who know of a magic user who lives outside of town. They are talented at taming feral creatures and turning them into familiars. Characters now draw this magic user's small dwelling on the map. These two PCs can pay the magic user to train creatures for them, but the cost is somewhat high or there are favors to be done.

For the Campaign (optional non-linear subplot) - Magic user tries to take something they cannot control and it eats them (or most of them—legs and an arm) / magic user is captured and made to tame creatures for a villain.

D10 Fortune or Misfortune

1. Choose two characters who found a weird pile of foreign coins one night. GM points to the map and characters draw where they found the pile. There are 6D6 coins. GM decides where they are from and who might have owned them. Characters decide who carries this odd money or if they split it.

For the Campaign (optional non-linear subplot) - Coins are cured / coins belong to a magic user who can track PCs using the coins / when coins are used, the person who received them falls sick / coins are more valuable to an NPC the party meets later in the campaign.

2. Choose three characters who were out one night at an inn or tavern. Have the characters draw this place on the map. They were gambling that night. Have them all roll initiative. The highest character won a modest pot of money as well as an attack dog that does not want to leave town. It's loyal to the players, but always sleeps under a large tree. Characters now draw this tree on the map.

For the Campaign (optional non-linear subplot) - Attack dog can lead party to unexplored areas and track down enemies / attack dog grows increasingly hostile until its loyalty is gone and attacks the party / attack dog often attacks NPCs that it thinks are threats to the party.

3. Choose two characters who found a small book of magic when they were a little younger. Neither of them can read it and no local person understands the language inside. Have the characters draw the location on the map where they found the book—it must be outside of the town/city. GM decides if this book's secrets are ever revealed. Characters roll initia-

tive and the highest character has the book in their possession.

For the Campaign (optional non-linear subplot) - Book belonged to an NPC of the GM's choice / book is cursed / book gives a glimpse into the future (campaign) or an alternate world.

4. Choose two characters that encountered a plagued NPC who was wandering around. Have both characters roll initiative. The slowest rolled character is sick and will need help from an NPC that the GM creates.

For the Campaign (optional non-linear subplot) - The cause of the plague is a magic user / plague causes lasting effects (maybe not harmful to stats, but are aesthetically unpleasing).

5. Choose two characters who both went to the same party one night. Have one of the characters draw where the party was on the map. One of these two characters of your choice insulted an NPC and this person/creature hasn't forgiven them. It's up to the GM as to how important this NPC is to the campaign. The party was also pretty epic. Characters might have met new friends or love interests there.

For the Campaign (optional non-linear subplot) - NPC has important information that can unlock an area of the map / NPC is a family member of another NPC that was already created in this book.

6. Choose two characters who were ambushed one night. They were badly hurt and lost a few important items, but a local NPC helped them once the bandits were gone. Characters now draw the location where they were attacked on the map as well as the location of the friendly NPC's house.

For the Campaign (optional non-linear subplot) - Bandits can be tracked down because the friendly NPC knows who they are / friendly NPC is affiliated with the bandits and is only trying to make the party more vulnerable to future attacks.

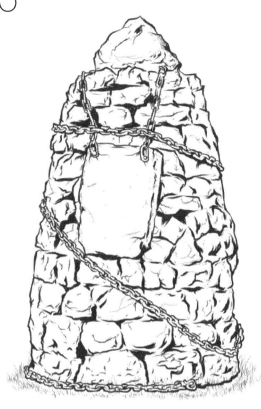

7. Choose two characters who befriend a low level magic user who comes to their aide once in a while—teleporting—and then disappearing without explanation. Have the two characters draw where this magic user lives on the map.

For the Campaign (optional non-linear subplot) - Magic user is influenced by a villain or NPC with conflicting motivations / magic user is kind of a jerk / magic user is in love with a PC of the GM's choosing.

8. Choose two characters that were ambushed and abducted one night by a roving gang of bandits. All their belongings were taken. A nearby NPC witnessed the ambush, but had no means of helping. They know where the bandits are located. These two characters must be rescued.

For the Campaign (optional non-linear subplot) - An NPC that has already been created by this book is part of the bandit gang / if located, the gang has all the stolen items plus more as well as a clue to a side-quest.

9. Choose two characters who found a large egg. It hatches.

For the Campaign (optional non-linear subplot) - Egg has a familiar inside: 1D6: 1 reptile, 2 bird of prey, 3 amphibian, 4 mammal, 5 fish, 6 magic being / egg has a deadly creature inside / egg belongs to an NPC that was already created by this book / egg belongs to a villain and they will hunt it down once it hatches.

10. Choose two characters that find a magic wand.

For the Campaign (optional non-linear subplot) - Wand can be used by non-magic users and its not very powerful, but kind of useful / wand belongs to an NPC already created by this book / wand is very powerful, but cursed / wand attracts weird beings or creatures.

D10 Roads (use this once five or more locations have been drawn on the map)

1. Choose two locations that are now joined by a road. Choose a character that hasn't had a turn drawing in a while and have them draw the road on the map. There are a few trading posts along the road that the character must draw as well and they can dictate, along with the GM, what these trading posts sell. One of these locations might be owned by an NPC that was already created by this book.

2. Choose two locations that are now joined by a road. Choose a character that hasn't had a turn drawing in a while and have them draw the road on the map. This road is treacherous—bandits have been known to ambush travelers. The character that drew this road has a history with one of the bandit leaders. The GM decides what that history is.

3. Choose two locations that are now joined by a road. Choose a character that hasn't had a turn drawing in a while and have them draw the road on the map. This character lost an item of the GM's choosing while traveling along this route and an NPC that has already been created found the item. The character can choose to get it back.

4. Choose two locations that are now joined by a road. Choose a character that hasn't had a turn drawing in a while and have them draw the road on the map. An NPC that has already been created used to own a toll along this road and they collected money for a local baron. Now that the baron is recently dead, the toll is inactive, but locals resent

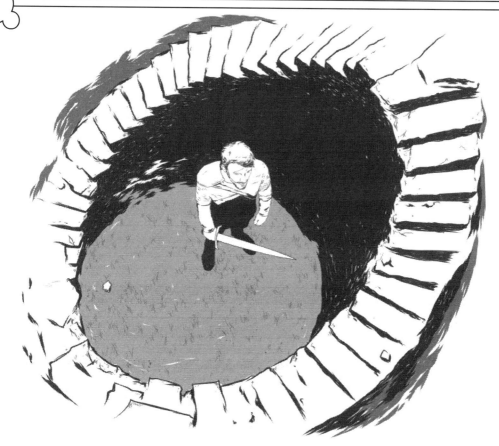

the NPC for taking money from them for years. GM can decide if this NPC will be attacked because of their affiliation with the baron.

5. Choose two locations that are now joined by a road. Choose a character that hasn't had a turn drawing in a while and have them draw the road on the map. There are two prominent buildings along this road which the GM must create. One of them is hostile to the party and one of them is friendly.

6. Choose two locations that are now joined by a road that also forks in the middle and leads to a wooded area. Choose a character that hasn't had a turn drawing in a while and have them draw the road on the map. Inside this wooded area is a hideout that the character has used in the past. They now draw this on the map and, if the character wants, a more detailed half-page drawing of the hideout in the back of the book.

7. Choose two locations that are now joined by a road. Choose a character that hasn't had a turn drawing in a while and have them draw the road on the map. Some kind of massacre or disaster occurred recently leaving half a dozen dead along with three dead horses and one injured horse. Their weapons and loot have been stolen. Character can keep the injured horse though it is now somewhat untrusting of humans. No one knows what happened except for an NPC that has already been generated by this book.

8. Choose two locations that are now joined by a road. Choose a character that hasn't had a turn drawing in a while and have them draw the road on the map. There's a broken cart blocking the road and it's loaded with goods of the GM's choosing. Anyone that helps the owner of the cart get back on their route might be rewarded. GM can also dictate where the owner of the cart is going and choose a character to draw this location on the map if it does not exist yet.

9. Choose two locations that are now joined by a road. Choose a character that hasn't had a turn drawing in a while and have them draw the road on the map. Part of this road was swallowed by a sinkhole that might or might not be a den for creatures. Character draws this modest size sinkhole.

10. Choose two locations that are now joined by a road. Choose a character that hasn't had a turn drawing in a while and have them draw the road on the map. An NPC who was delivering good to a local noble person was robbed by bandits along this road. If his belongings are recovered, the noble will reward the party.

D10 Landmarks (use this once five or more locations have been drawn on the map)

First roll 1D4 for north = 1 / east = 2 / south = 3 / west = 4. If you do not want the characters to know what these landmarks are, just mark the map with a symbol and write that symbol and a description of the location in the book.

1. There's an abandoned tower in the (1D4) region of the map. An NPC that has already been generated by the book knows about it and why it's there.

2. There's a mass grave in the (1D4) region of the map. An NPC that has already been generated by the book knows about it and why it's there.

3. There's a burning house in the (1D4) region of the map. An NPC that has already been generated by the book has family that owns the house.

4. There's a buried crypt in the (1D4) region of the map. An NPC of the GM's choosing knows what the mystery is.

5. There's a gaming den in the (1D4) region of the map. An NPC of the GM's choosing goes there a lot, but their family does not know. This person is in a lot of debt and will be in peril next time they gamble and lose.

6. There's a mysterious cult's church in the (1D4) region of the map. An NPC of the GM's choosing worships there, in secret.

7. There's a field in the (1D4) region of the map. People who go there at night sometimes never come back. An NPC of the GM's choosing knows what the mystery is.

8. There's a farm in the (1D4) region of the map. Cannibals live there. They keep a cellar filled with dismembered people they are slowly eating. An NPC of the GM's choice has a family member who is missing—they're in the cellar.

9. There's an old well in the (1D4) region of the map. Locals say there's something inside—either a winding crypt or dungeon.

10. There's an armorer or weapon smith who lives in the (1D4)

region of the map. An NPC that has already been generated by this book can introduce the party to this person.

D10 Wildlife

1. Flocks of winged animals inhabit an area of the map. They're terribly annoying to an NPC.

2. Wild dogs or wolves are attacking children in an area of the map.

3. Some of the most delicious fish in the land can be found in a remote section of a river.

4. Biting insects make a section of the map unfriendly to the party at night, but an NPC knows how to inoculate PCs against them.

5. Wild horses roam an area of the map and an NPC is an expert at breaking them.

6. A few groundhogs have burrowed underneath an NPC's house and are compromising the dwelling's foundation as well as eating all the surrounding crops.

7. A creature roams the area and their fur can be used by a local herbalist to create powerful potions.

8. An endangered species exists in a remote area of the map and an NPC is highly invested in preserving them.

9. An NPC is crossbreeding two animals and the results are strange and/or dangerous. They might be tamed as familiars as well.

10. Lice live on livestock in the area. They carry diseases that affect PC's stats or abilities.

D12 Neighboring Towns and Cities

1. A close by town is plentiful with something that the party lacks, but hostile NPCs control this item/good.

2. A neighboring village was attacked last night, leaving only a handful of people alive. They fled to the closest place on the map and are seeking shelter. GM can create the threat who attacked them or leave it a mystery. The village is mostly burned, but can be reclaimed at the party's own risk.

3. Choose an NPC that has already been created by this book that needs to be escorted to a neighboring town. They are carrying something valuable and are willing to pay for help.

4. The population of a neighboring town or city hates the residents of the town or city that the party is from. These people visit once in a while to fight, but it's usually non-deadly. GM can name them and give them a motivation if that contributes to the story in a meaningful way.

5. A nearby town or city is well-known in the area for a colony of armorers, but they create their armor from a creature that only roams the area around the party's map. The armorers hunt these creatures, but the locals are unhappy about this activity.

6. A neighboring town or city sits upriver from the party's area. Residents of this location are polluting the river and it's creating strife among the locals, especially people situated closest to the pollution.

7. A mountain sits somewhat nearby where a colony of hermetic people somehow survive. They are expert hunters and create inventive weapons from local resources. An NPC that has already been created by this book knows of their location and has befriended a family there.

8. A series of hills is nestled not far from the area. The folks that live there do not speak, but have an uncanny connection to their environment and the wildlife. They are friendly if traded with.

9. Volcanic activity occurs somewhere in the area. Locals use hot springs and this location has become a secret destination for travelers. The rocks of this area can be used to create both exotic weapons and potions, but dangerous creatures stalk the land.

10. A neighboring village was accidentally settled on a network of underground tunnels which have recently collapsed, leaving many dead. Many people in the party's town/city have connections to the dead people from this village. A malicious NPC is responsible for the tragedy.

11. A nearby town or city has kept slaves for generations, but not anymore—the slaves revolted and murdered their masters. Anyone left alive fled to the party's town/city and are seeking help. The party will have to decide whose side they are on.

12. A neighboring village or town is ravaged by a drug addiction that is killing its population. An NPC that was already created by this book is also addicted to this drug and is spreading it around in the party's town/city. It is highly addictive and temporarily increases stats, but at a high cost.

D6 Betrayal of Friends

Warning. Only use this section if you want potentially severe conflict between your party.

1. Choose two characters, one of which divulged a weakness or secret of the other character to a stranger while drunk. This was a simple mistake that could lead to dire consequences. Maybe a villain has spies in the area and they now have knowledge of this character's weakness or secret.

2. Choose two characters, one of which "borrowed" an item from the other character and they have not returned it yet.

3. Choose two characters, one of which is now romantically involved with a lover or ex-lover of the other character. This is a secret. GM can whisper this into the romantically involved character's ear or write it down on a slip of paper so the other character does not know. Rumors might spread about this relationship.

4. Choose two characters, one of which promised the other character they would do something extremely important for them, but didn't follow through. This could be delivering a letter, taking care of a sick loved one, feeding a pet (familiar), watching over a property, or anything personal that would greatly affect the other character.

5. Choose two characters, one of which accidentally insulted the other character's appearance or something deeper like their motivation for being part of the group. The character who insulted the other might have been just joking around, but the words were taken seriously and will have a lasting effect.

6. Choose two characters, one of which borrowed a valuable item from the other and lost it. It's gone forever.

D6 Besties for Life

Members of your party can easily be best friends. Tight bonds are made when adventuring together.

1. Choose two characters who co-own a large and trusty steed. This horse can be very handy in battle or travel. This horse is on the older side and near the end of its life, though it is still extraordinarily strong.

2. Choose two characters who share a secret—any secret about the area that provides them with an advantage, but potentially harms other characters or just NPCs. This can be a recourse that only the two characters know about or an NPC that is taking advantage of the population while giving favor to the characters.

3. Choose two characters who are good friends with a baron or lord from a neighboring area. This NPC can send packages and even armed guards if needed. Some NPCs the party will encounter will hate this NPC and they will not trust any character who is associated with them.

4. Choose two characters that share an addiction to something somewhat harmful, but downright fun: a substance, an activity, or maybe an NPC that they both like a lot.

5. Choose two characters who created their own weird holiday that they celebrate each year. Coincidentally, this holiday is coming up!

6. Choose two characters who witnessed a tragedy together and it has not only shaped who they've become, but they occasionally bond over the shared memory.

D12 Weird Fun

1. Choose two characters who have a secret handshake that an NPC sees and thinks they have the same secret handshake.

2. Choose two characters who have the same birthday which will happen very soon.

3. Choose two characters who both got food poisoning from the same inn.

4. Choose two characters who slept with the same NPC who is famous for something very strange, yet useful to the party.

5. Choose two characters who are addicted to something non-harmful.

6. Choose two characters who share three rare wooden dice and regularly play a simple gambling game to pass the time.

7. Choose two characters who borrowed an NPC's boat and accidentally sank it—now they are avoiding this person or disagree about what to do. NPC is mad as hell.

8. Choose two characters who are allergic to a substance who both had close calls as kids—they almost died from this substance.

9. Choose two characters who both saw some strange, unexplainable phenomenon in the night's sky and one other NPC saw it too.

10. Choose two characters who have been asked to pet sit for an NPC who will be away for a month. The pet is kind of mean.

11. Choose two characters who got their fortune read by the same NPC. One character's future was bright. The other... not so much. This could foretell something that will happen in the campaign.

12. Choose two characters who are being pursued by a magical being who is infatuated with them.

D100 Location Attributes

Have your characters draw some of these on the map. Re-roll if you roll the same number twice.

1. Recently swarmed by insects that caused a lasting poison effect.
2. Livestock use a close by path, sometimes attracting predators.
3. A person who sells simple games and wooden sculptures is often seen around here.
4. Delicious berry bushes growing nearby.
5. Cats are attracted to this place.
6. This is a spot where gamblers set up a makeshift camp once in a while.
7. Food spoils quickly here for some unknown reason.
8. An attractive person walks by here once a day.
9. An unmarked headstone stands in a north facing part of the property or nearby.
10. Lightning has struck a nearby tree three times in the past year.
11. Mites infest all bedding here and/or nearby.
12. A magic user's apprentice forages for ingredients in this area.
13. A family died nearby and is said to haunt this location at night.
14. Witches have been seen recently in this area.
15. There is an abundance of a food source nearby.
16. Dogs are spooked by this place.
17. Some say there is an underground labyrinth close by.
18. A roaming creature has been spotted twice at dusk.
19. Set along a secret route of traveling sex workers.
20. Small/medium size familiars will not go near this place as there have been sightings of large, roaming creatures.
21. Some magic tends to have a reverse affect when cast in this place.
22. Someone has set a trap nearby.
23. A modest amount of money is found on the ground.
24. Useful herbs grow nearby.
25. Something metal is half-buried in the ground.
26. Someone who people call Pig Dog walks by here often wearing a thick brown hooded cloak.
27. An elaborate rainwater collection system is here or nearby.
28. Cannibals occupied this place once. People still talk about it.
29. Drought. It hasn't rained in some time and any water stored

here is gone.

30. There's a small cave nearby with someone living in it.
31. Always damp. Wood rots quickly here if not cared for.
32. There is a well nearby that many people use.
33. An assassin has been seen training their teenager in a close by field.
34. A wrecked wagon is now a play space for children.
35. There is a view of the sunset from here that will take your breath away.
36. An armorer lives close by and walks to the tavern every night.
37. A recent earthquake opened a large pit not far from here and rumors are circulating about what is inside.
38. A neighbor pretty much hates everyone, but he is very talented at something the party could use.
39. There's a plentiful garden close to this location that a few people tend.
40. A community meeting space isn't far from here.
41. Nearby, there is a large tree where noisy birds sleep at night.
42. A curse was cast on a nearby and subtle landmark.
43. Loud, bickering neighbors come and go throughout the night.
44. A brewer of beer or mead or the like lives close by.
45. There's a stash of weapons not far from here.
46. A horse recently died here and is rotting. Something is in its saddle.
47. All that's left is a stone foundation of a neighboring property—and three skeletons.
48. A popular realistic painter lives nearby.
49. A well known battle occurred nearby and not long ago—items to be found.
50. A terrible musician lives next door or close by.
51. There's a wedding schedule nearby of two popular people in the community.
52. Some types of magic are weakened here by a strange and unknown source.
53. A giant or very large person ran drunkenly into a tree and suffered fatal wounds.

54. An inventor lives close by and will ramble about their latest creation.
55. A trap expert lives not far from here and is willing to trade for their knowledge.
56. Someone recently committed suicide nearby.
57. Peasants always seems to wander around here looking for food.
58. An expert crossbow maker lives not to far from here.
59. A costume maker lives nearby and loves to barter.
60. Unusually large nocturnal flying mammals fly around here.
61. An expert of languages lives close by.
62. An expert tailor lives not far from here and is willing to barter.
63. Toxic groundwater seeps up and floods this area from time to time.
64. Someone says there's a talking animal that appears at night nearby.
65. People gather close to this location to play simple tabletop games.
66. A poisonous plant grows wild in this area.
67. A local cartographer lives close by and is willing to trade.
68. Someone claims to be a healer and they live not far from here.
69. A person or being has a special talent that can be learned at a high cost.
70. Someone set a trap nearby—a pit or snare.
71. A person with exotic goos will be driving their wagon through this area soon.
72. Musicians live nearby and they practice loudly some nights.
73. A bandit was caught and now they hang—dead—from a tree.
74. Someone piled several human skulls close by.
75. A large crack in the land zigzags north. People are afraid of what might lurk inside.
76. People are cutting down trees nearby, but bandits keep robbing them.
77. Mushrooms grow here and they have strange effects when eaten.
78. A wagon broke down nearby and the owner needs help.
79. A local blade sharpener can be of help and lives close by.
80. Close by, someone who is a trained singer is willing to teach their craft.
81. Something is rotting down a path and drawing large animals.

82. A sinkhole appears close to here, revealing an underground cave system.
83. The sap from a nearby tree is very sticky and can be useful.
84. Neighbors love to party, but dislike a certain race.
85. A fortuneteller lives down the road and is somewhat well known.
86. Acrobats practice their skills in a nearby field or open space.
87. Putrid stench wafts from a nearby bog.
88. A local magic user lives close by and can teach new spells.
89. Hostile creatures nest somewhat close to here.
90. There's a speakeasy of sorts close to here.
91. A demon is said to roam this area at night.
92. Children often play nearby and they usually have news to tell about the locals.
93. Evidence of a summoning circle in the dirt: crystals, a skull, drawn symbols.
94. Someone keeps horses fenced in close by, but two were stolen recently.
95. A neighbor and farmer makes the best goat cheese.
96. Someone close by will trade for giving wild haircuts and piercings.
97. A furniture maker has a workshop nearby.
98. A spell book is hidden nearby.
99. Gold is buried nearby.
100. A powerful weapon is hidden nearby.

D10 Deadly Location Attributes

1. Large, poisonous plants are overtaking the area, causing locals to get sick and ruining crops. A magical source is creating this wicked flora to grow.

2. Something is causing earthquakes that are decimating dwellings—the source might live deep below.

3. An underground spring is leeching poisonous water and flooding the area. Something ominous lives beneath.

4. High winds make living in this area especially hazardous though something magical might be causing them.

5. The trees in this part of the map are oddly "aggressive"—they reach out and snag people and sometimes they whip limbs and severely hurt people that are passing by. Some kind of magical influence is occurring.

6. People have reported spontaneous fires flaring up in this part of the map and no one can explain why.

7. Stones come alive, rolling and damaging property, even sometimes forming into elemental rock-like beings. There must be some sort of magic controlling them.

8. An acid-like rain seems to roll through this area once in a while and locals blame a nearby NPC who might be using magic. It severely damages all exposed metal.

9. A novice necromancer is reanimating the undead in this area

and even though this NPC might not be evil, they are inadvertently summoning hordes.

10. A dragon is attracted to this area because it is targeting a playable character's property. Its level will be +5 to the average level of the party. An NPC will know of a weakness that can disable the dragon.

Drop Tables (use this once five or more locations have been drawn on the map)

This is a great way for your party to meet for the first time if they haven't had a unified motivation to team up. One player rolls 2D6 on the map. If a die or both dice roll off the map, re-roll both dice. When rolling these dice, a "drop roll" is best so that—ideally—the dice bounce off each other and create a truly random outcome. Roll 1D10 to determine what event occurred after drop-rolling the 2D6 on the map:

1. The die that landed closest to a location marks the location that is affected. That die also indicates how much of a disadvantage people had when they were attacked (a roll of a four means they have a -4 on all rolls). The other die indicates how many people attacked that location and where they came from.

2. Both dice represent two opposing groups (the number indicating how many people/beings or single person/being if a die is 1) that charged each other and fought. GM names both groups and gives them characteristics and stats if needed. Slide both dice together to determine where the fight occurred. GM determines who won the fight, who witnessed the fight, and how the area was effected. Property that was in the vicinity of the battle might have been damaged or destroyed. If both numbers are the same, roll again.

3. Highest die is a large creature that is roaming the area. The number on that die is its level. GM assigns stats and traits to the creature. The lowest die is the creature's target or what it is hunting. The number on that die is the number of people it is after. GM determines who those lower number people are and if they have any relation to an NPC that was already generated by this book. If both numbers are the same, roll again.

4. Both dice represent buildings that are being constructed where they landed. They are owned by the same person: an overbearing lord who seeks to spread their influence. GM can name this lord and give them motivations. They might also be hiring local workers at a very low rate and some of them are getting injured. The numbers on the dice represent how many X 1,000 gold (or system equivalent) the property will be worth—if you rolled a 6 then the property is worth 6,000. If there are any nearby locations, they could be negatively affected by these new properties.

5. Both dice represent opposing legions that are rushing to battle. The numbers on the dice represent the level at which all fighters are. There is a somewhat equal number of fighters on each side and the GM dictates that number. GM can give each legion alliances with existing NPCs and the party can decide if they wish to aide a side in battle. GM slides both dice together in a centered location where the battle occurs. If the dice slid over any properties, they could have been affected by the roving legion.

6. Have all players roll initiative and keep in mind who rolled the lowest number. Now drop-roll the 2D6 on the map. Add +2 to each die number to represent how many beings have spawned where the dice landed. Both dice represent the same threat: feral creatures or roving bandits or whatever NPCs would make sense within the narrative you've already established. Both groups are walking to a central point where the two dice meet when slid together. They are meeting there to plan an attack against the character who rolled the lowest in initiative. GM decides what this NPC group's motivation is.

7. In the center of both dice is where something crawled out of the ground. It peeled in two—slug-like and hulking, and crawled in the directions of the two dice. Where the dice landed is where the slug-like creatures stopped and devoured people. The number of people is the number on the dice. These creatures then burrowed back into the earth. They can rise again if the GM chooses, this time eating X 2 the number of people ditched by the dice.

8. Where the dice landed, GM draws as symbols marking: highest die is where loot/treasure is hidden or buried and the lowest die is where bodies are hidden/buried. These people were killed by an unknown NPC and they stashed the raided loot. GM should keep this a secret until the players search these two new locations.

9. Where the dice landed mark where people have been mysteriously killed. The numbers on the dice are how many people were murdered. The character who owns property or is closest to the highest number die will be blamed by some people in the community. The GM can create NPCs who are blaming the character and also the real NPC/creature that murdered the 2D6 people.

10. An NPC that the party knows can tell them about neighboring places. Using the center of the map as a starting point, each die represents a direction a new location exists. The number on the die represents the miles or kilometers one must travel to get there. GM decides what lies at these locations, but they must add backstory to at least two characters.

Area Attacked

This is another great way for your party to meet for the first time if they haven't had a unified motivation to team up. One player rolls 2D8 on the map. If a die or both dice roll off the map, re-roll both dice. When rolling these dice, a "drop roll" is best so that—ideally—the dice bounce off each other and create a truly random outcome. The highest die represents the level (+1) of the creature that is attacking. The lowest die represents an NPC that is being attacked and the number on the die represents their level. Party can come to their rescue. The closest property to the lowest die is in jeopardy and will be damaged or destroyed in the attack. If the level of the creature is very high, the NPC who is being attacked can also have high stats to compensate for the imbalance. NPC may reward party with loot if they are aided. Roll 1D6 to determine the outcome of the NPC:

1. NPC will die in battle, leaving nothing because the creature destroyed the NPC's body and belongings.

2. NPC will die in battle, leaving only what they have on them as loot.

3. NPC will die in battle, leaving what was on their body as well as a map to their home.

4. NPC will barely survive in battle and ask to be carried to their home where they die within a few days without high-level magic healing.

5. NPC will barely survive in battle and ask to be carried to their home where they will survive, but not recover fully or have the same fighting capacity as before. Party is rewarded modestly.

6. NPC will survive the battle and fully recover. They invite the party back to their home and the party is rewarded handsomely.

Random Drops

Drop-roll 6D4 on the map. These are where a rogue set traps overnight. GM should keep the nature of these a secret to the characters.

Drop 2D20 on the map. The highest die is the level of a weapon that is hidden where the die landed. The lowest die is the level and location of the NPC who knows how to uncover the mysterious weapon. GM keeps all of this a secret until party investigates.

Drop 2D6 on the Map until only one of them lands on a dwelling. The die that landed on the dwelling is the number of thieves stealing as much as they can from the place. The other D6 are the NPCs related to that dwelling and where they are (with friends if the number on the die is high). Someone will alert the party that this dwelling is being broken into.

Drop 2D20 on the map. The highest number is the level and location of a magic user who is attempting to conjure a familiar. The lowest number die is the familiar's location and level. If both numbers are the same, re-roll.

Drop 2D20 on the map. The highest number is the location of a bard who is about to set up for the night to sing. The number on that die is the number of songs they will preform. The number on the other D20 is the location and amount of NPCs who are on their way to see this bard perform. The higher number of NPCs, the better mood this bard will be in. He is a happy bard, they might be useful to the party. If they are unhappy, they might be a pest.

D10 Abominations Abound

Use this section when your party has established much if not all of their map and backstory.

1. Drop-roll 1D20 and 2D6 in the center of the map and make sure they ricochet off each other. The D20 is a dragon and the level of that dragon. Where the dice landed is where the dragon now sits, recovering from its sudden arrival. The 2D6s are the number of dead warriors/wizards/elves etc (other party members) it deposited in the town/city. Their smoldering bodies are hot enough to stick to wherever they landed. Characters can decide to engage the dragon if they wish. GM decides if this dragon has a lair close by with loot or gold.

2. Drop-roll 1D20 and 3D6 in the center of the map and make sure they ricochet off each other. The D20 is a Serpent Queen and the level that she is. Where the D20 landed is where her underground lair is. The 3D6s are openings in the tunnel network where the Queen can send out minions. The numbers on the D6s represent the number of minions that guard each tunnel opening. GM is free to create a secret underground tunnel map that matches these openings as well as where the Queen's lair is and if it contains loot or gold. The map can be as simple or complex as the GM wishes. Locations close to the tunnel openings may be affected.

3. Drop-roll 1D20 and 2D10 in the center of the map and make sure they ricochet off each other. The D20 is a giant griffin that has landed in the area and the number on the D20 is its level. The 2D10 are NPCs who were battling the griffin and

were clinging to its feathers. They got some damaging strikes in before it took to the air and dumped them. Now the NPCs are badly hurt and, as the griffin regroups, it will hunt them down.

4. Drop-roll 2D10 and 2D6 in the center of the map and make sure they ricochet off each other. The 2D10 are giant ogres who are slowly trampling through the area. The numbers on the D10s are their levels. The 2D6 are groups of local warriors (all equal to the party's average level) who are arming themselves to fight the ogres. The numbers on the 2D6 are the num-

bers of NPCs in those groups. Both ogres will charge the closest group and slaughter them all. The second group will come
to their rescue. Each ogre carries a considerable amount of loot.

5. Drop-roll 2D20 in the center of the map and make sure they
ricochet off each other. The lowest number D20 is a massive great
sword that fell from the sky and is stuck in the ground. It is over
50 feet high. The highest number D20 is a group of people (D20
x 2 people) who have come to worship it as a sign from their god.
Once they are at the base of the sword, a giant knight will come
to retrieve it. The knight is the level of the party's average +2.
The knight will slay all the worshipers as they bow and scream.
Once the knight is done slaying the worshipers, it will chuck its
sword in the air as high as it can throw, making it land miles away.

6. Drop-roll 6D6 in the center of the map and make sure they
ricochet off each other. Each die represents the number of undead soldiers that a necromancer is reanimating from unmarked
graves. They will convene to the highest number die (if there are
two or more highest number dice, GM decides where they will
convene). They are -2 level of the average level of the party. Lowest number die can reveal a crypt where loot was buried/stashed.

7. Drop-roll 4D6 in the center of the map and make sure they
ricochet off each other. The dice represent four magic users who
appeared one night and are casting a field spell. Each die represents their level, where they stand, and the corners of the field.
Anything inside the field is paralyzed unless they are a magic user
who can fight this spell. Anything outside the field suffers from an
abysmal ringing in their ears, but they are otherwise fine. Inside
the field, a massive rock-like elemental beast rises. It is a high
level NPC, but it relies on the magic users for its animation and
powers. In the center of this beast is a mass of precious metal.

8. Drop-roll 4D6 in the center of the map and make sure they
ricochet off each other. The highest number die is the base of

a tower that has risen out of the ground. MG stacks the rest of
the dice on the base in order of numbers (lowest on the bottom,
highest number die on the top). This stack represents a four-sto-
ry tower and the numbers on the dice represent how many cham-
bers are in each story. The tower is accessible from the base and
within the tower are minions inside each story who are -2 levels of
the average level of the party. At the top of the tower is a magic
user who is +2 of the average level of the party. The magic user
will be after an NPC who was already created by this book. If the
party does not explore the tower, the magic user will send out
minions to abduct this NPC and bring them to the tower. Once
they do, the tower will descend into the ground and disappear.

9. Drop-roll 4D6 and 1D4 in the center of the map and make sure they ricochet off each other. The center-most D6 is the base of a stone chapel that appeared overnight. The D4 is the top of the chapel. The number on the D4 is the level of the magic user who lives in this weird house. The remaining D6s are smaller stone houses and the numbers on the dice represent the number of low-level magic users (disciples) that live there. They all worship a sorcerer who occupies the central chapel. The disciples will venture out and try to recruit townspeople into their cult. If the sorcerer is not stopped, the town/city will fall to their influence.

10. Drop-roll 2D10 in the center of the map and make sure they ricochet off each other. The highest D10 is a giant demon that has been summoned. The number on the D10 is its level. The lowest D10 is the magic user who summoned it and they are using the demon to attack a high-valued NPC and/or property.

Off Nights
Adding Non-Linear Subplots to Your Campaign

This section is a primer for adding content into your campaign to make it non-linear. For example, on an off-night, have your characters go back in time with this book and develop more of their backstory. This can happen mid-way through your main campaign to give you details and subplot to weave into the main story. The occasional off night can compound into even more meaningful content as your characters begin to care about things that not only happened in the past, but how they are actively affecting the "now."

If your characters have not all met yet to establish their group, an off night is a perfect way to create that unifying moment where they all came together. This could be a tragedy or event that means a lot to the town/city or it could be a battle that ended in the unification of your characters. Weaving in details of this event into the campaign can also add value to your overall story.

Even if they did establish how they all met during the first session of the book, you can still create a major event to unify them further or even to create new tensions within the group.

If your characters are about to meet an important NPC in the campaign, use an off night to go back in time to before the campaign and add in foreshadowing about this NPC. Maybe this NPC has influence over the town/city your characters created with this book.

It's common for new players to want to play in your campaign, but it's difficult to just drop new playable characters into a plot. On an off night, going back in time to a prequel setting allows you to create playable characters that can add meaningful content to your story. This will also let you reintroduce the same new playable character(s) into the campaign, making it possible for new players to jump in. And of course, you can kill them off when needed.

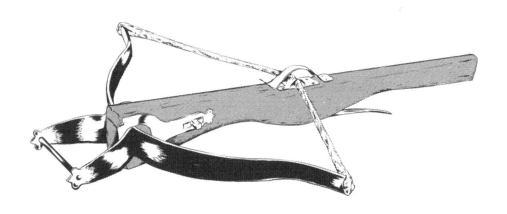

Compounding Relations
1D6 & 1D4

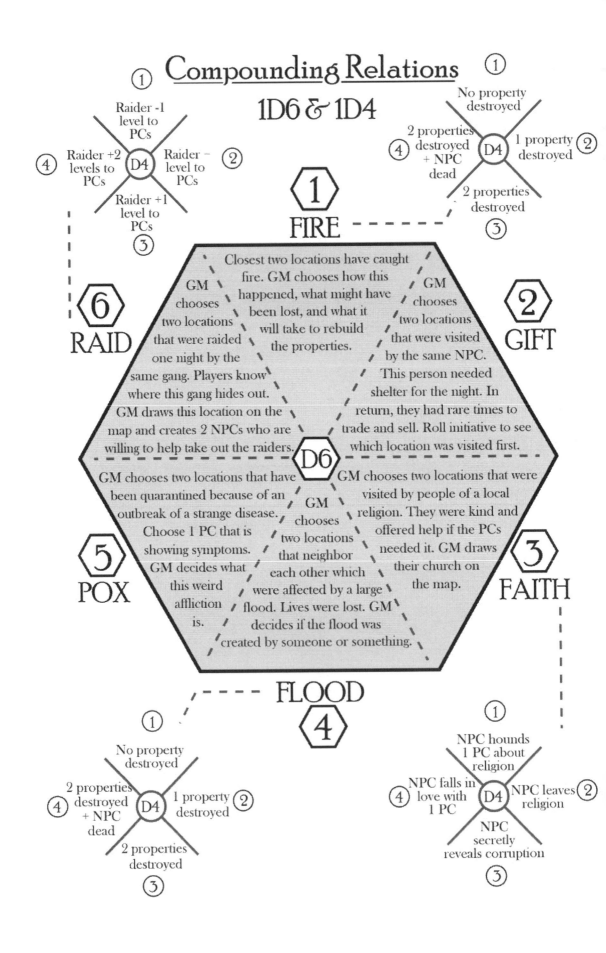

① FIRE

Closest two locations have caught fire. GM chooses how this happened, what might have been lost, and what it will take to rebuild the properties.

D4 (FIRE):
- ① No property destroyed
- ② 1 property destroyed
- ③ 2 properties destroyed
- ④ 2 properties destroyed + NPC dead

② GIFT

GM chooses two locations that were visited by the same NPC. This person needed shelter for the night. In return, they had rare times to trade and sell. Roll initiative to see which location was visited first.

③ FAITH

GM chooses two locations that were visited by people of a local religion. They were kind and offered help if the PCs needed it. GM draws their church on the map.

D4 (FAITH):
- ① NPC hounds 1 PC about religion
- ② NPC leaves religion
- ③ NPC secretly reveals corruption
- ④ NPC falls in love with 1 PC

④ FLOOD

GM chooses two locations that neighbor each other which were affected by a large flood. Lives were lost. GM decides if the flood was created by someone or something.

D4 (FLOOD):
- ① No property destroyed
- ② 1 property destroyed
- ③ 2 properties destroyed
- ④ 2 properties destroyed + NPC dead

⑤ POX

GM chooses two locations that have been quarantined because of an outbreak of a strange disease. Choose 1 PC that is showing symptoms. GM decides what this weird affliction is.

⑥ RAID

GM chooses two locations that were raided one night by the same gang. Players know where this gang hides out. GM draws this location on the map and creates 2 NPCs who are willing to help take out the raiders.

D4 (RAID):
- ① Raider -1 level to PCs
- ② Raider = level to PCs
- ③ Raider +1 level to PCs
- ④ Raider +2 levels to PCs

D6 (center)

1D12 NPCs 1. Priest 2. Witch 3. Noble 4. Squire 5. Baker 6. Farmer
7. Assassin 8. Inn Keeper 9. Knight 10. Wizard 11. Dwarf 12. Warrior

① Compounding Tensions
1D12 & 1D6 & 1D4

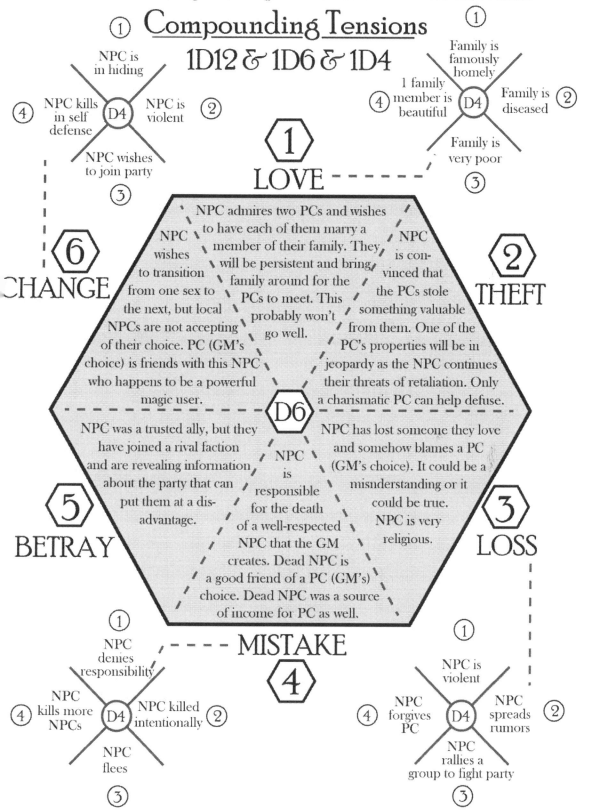

LOVE ①

NPC is in hiding ①
NPC is violent ②
NPC kills in self defense ④
NPC wishes to join party ③
D4

Family is famously homely ①
Family is diseased ②
Family is very poor ③
1 family member is beautiful ④
D4

⑥ CHANGE

② THEFT

NPC admires two PCs and wishes to have each of them marry a member of their family. They will be persistent and bring family around for the PCs to meet. This probably won't go well.

NPC wishes to transition from one sex to the next, but local NPCs are not accepting of their choice. PC (GM's choice) is friends with this NPC who happens to be a powerful magic user.

NPC is convinced that the PCs stole something valuable from them. One of the PC's properties will be in jeopardy as the NPC continues their threats of retaliation. Only a charismatic PC can help defuse.

D6

NPC was a trusted ally, but they have joined a rival faction and are revealing information about the party that can put them at a disadvantage.

NPC is responsible for the death of a well-respected NPC that the GM creates. Dead NPC is a good friend of a PC (GM's) choice. Dead NPC was a source of income for PC as well.

NPC has lost someone they love and somehow blames a PC (GM's choice). It could be a misunderstanding or it could be true. NPC is very religious.

⑤ BETRAY

③ LOSS

MISTAKE ④

NPC denies responsibility ①
NPC killed intentionally ②
NPC flees ③
NPC kills more NPCs ④
D4

NPC is violent ①
NPC spreads rumors ②
NPC rallies a group to fight party ③
NPC forgives PC ④
D4

Use the following map sections when you need to create a dungeon, crypt, maze, pit/trap, or village on the fly. There is no real symbol key because we want to keep this an open utility for you to interpret as you see fit. Skulls can symbolize enemies, arrows could be arrow traps, and circiles on the floor can either be pressure plates for doors/traps or markers for items. It's up to you.

There are also sections for your own custom drop tables and keys for any symbols you create.

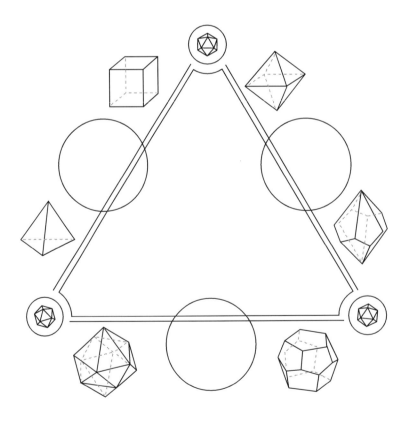

1D12 Dungeon Maze Sections

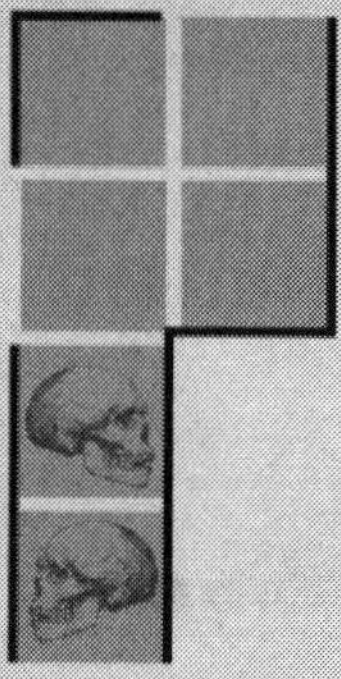

1

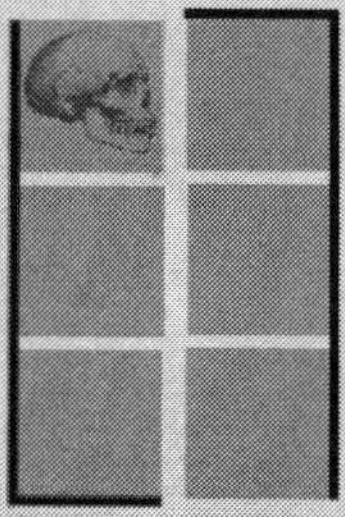

2

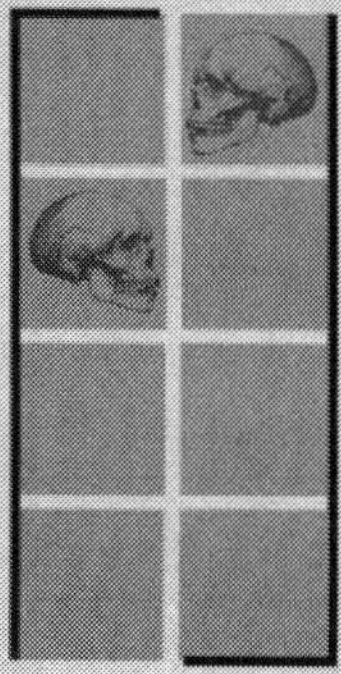

3

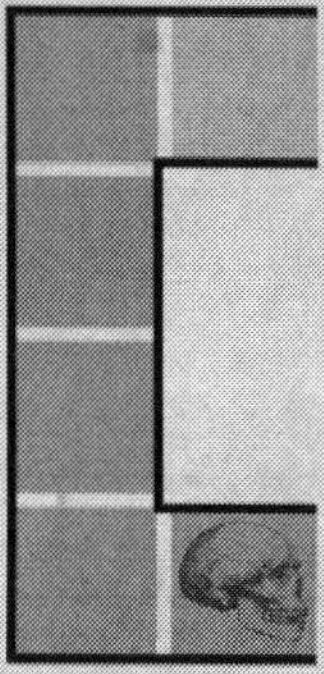

4

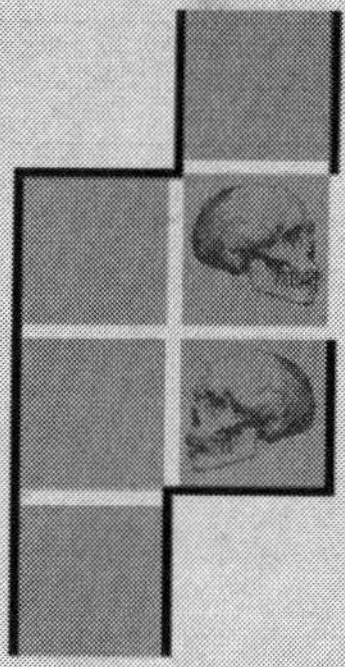

5

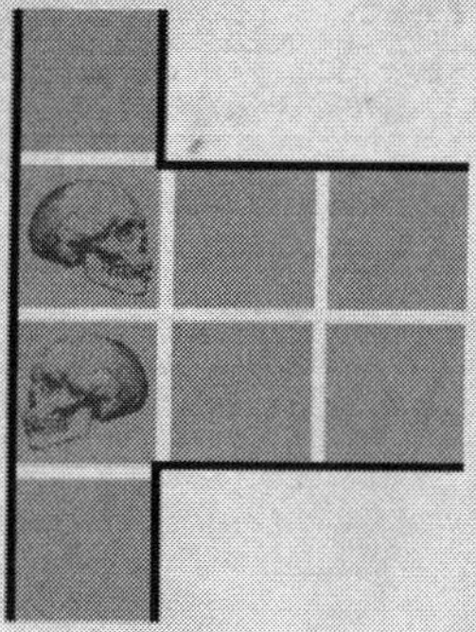

6

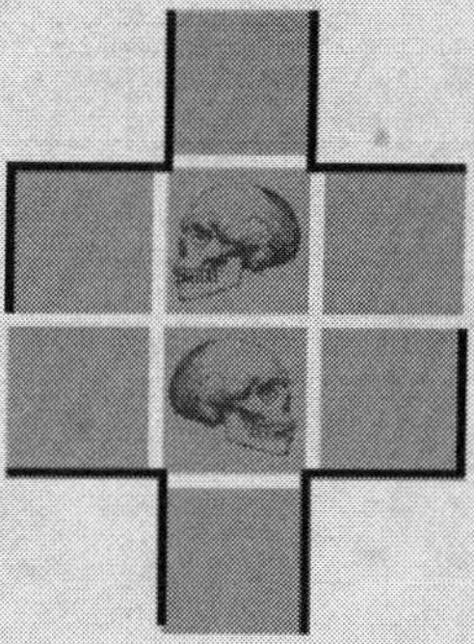

7

8

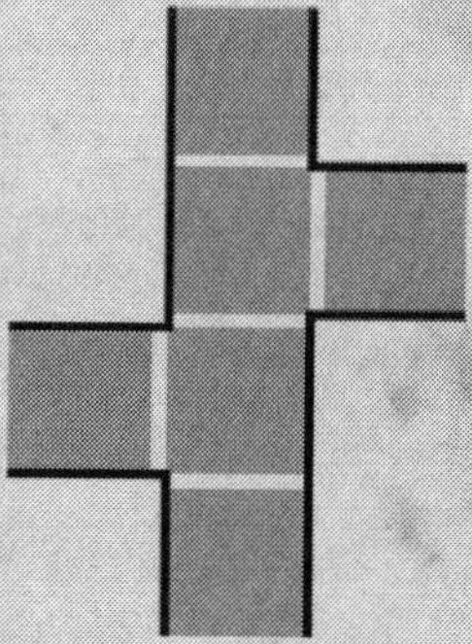

9

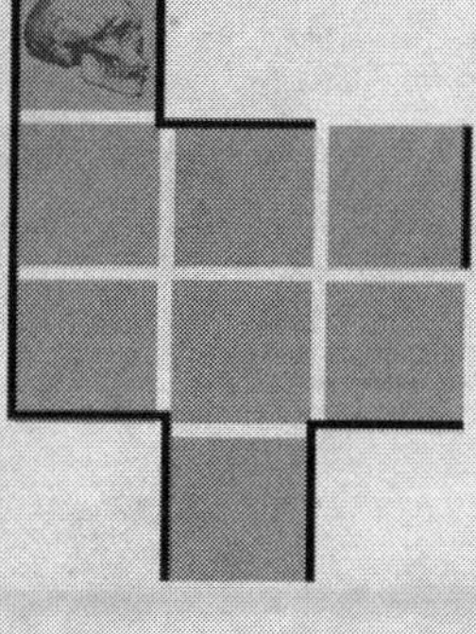

10

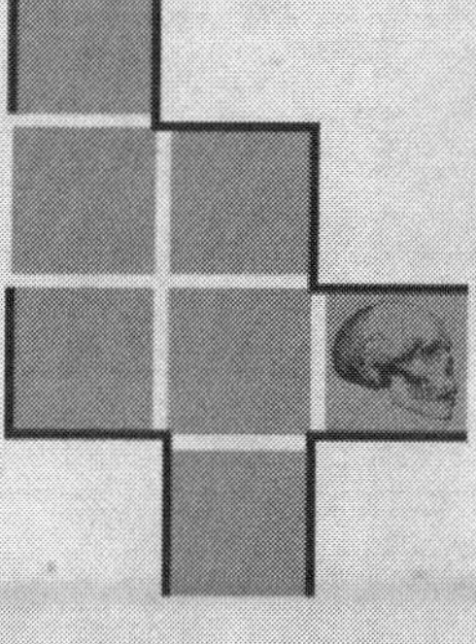

11

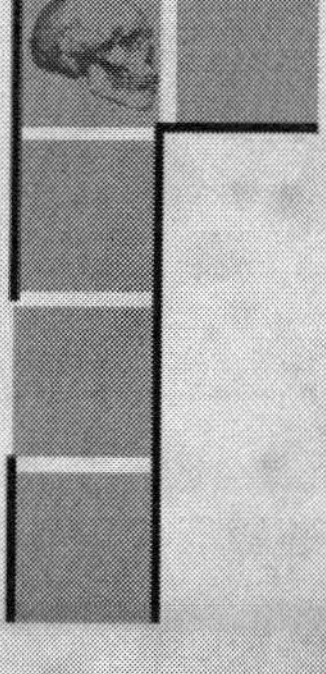

12

1D12 Dungeon Maze Sections

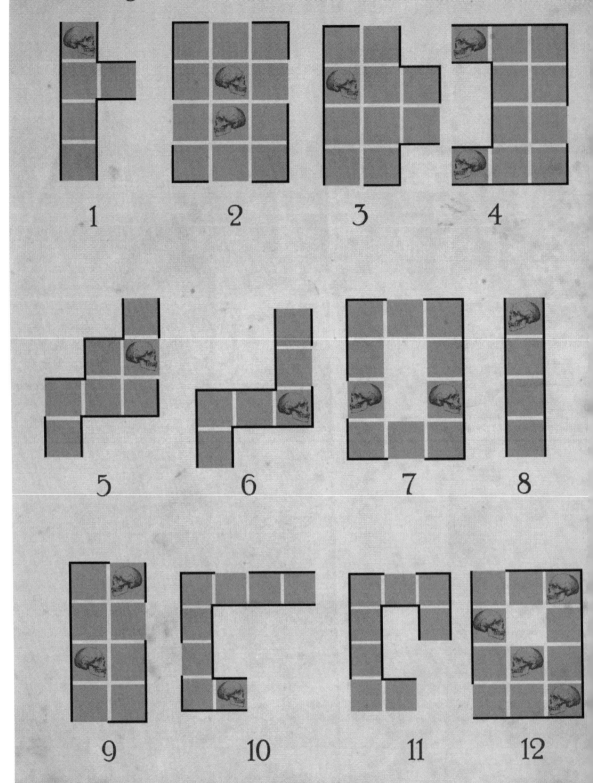

1

2

3

4

5

6

7

8

9

10

11

12

1D12 Dungeon Maze Sections

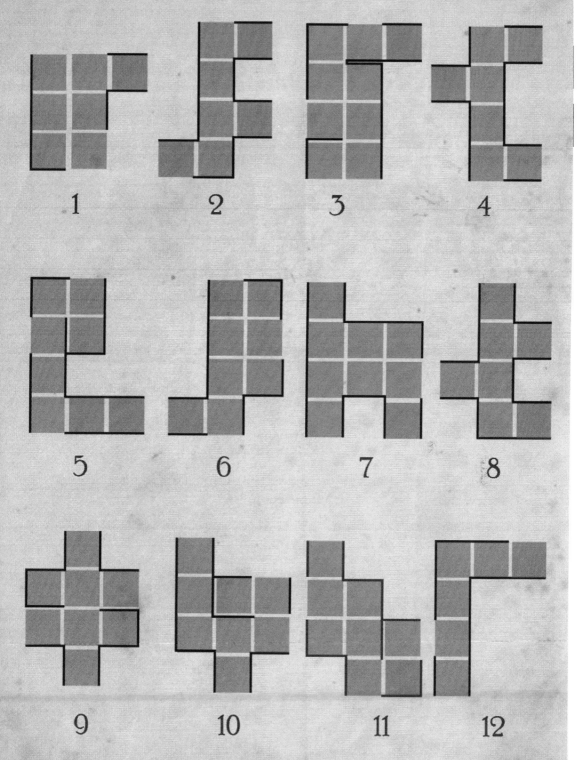

1

2

3

4

5

6

7

8

9

10

11

12

1D12 Dungeon Maze Sections

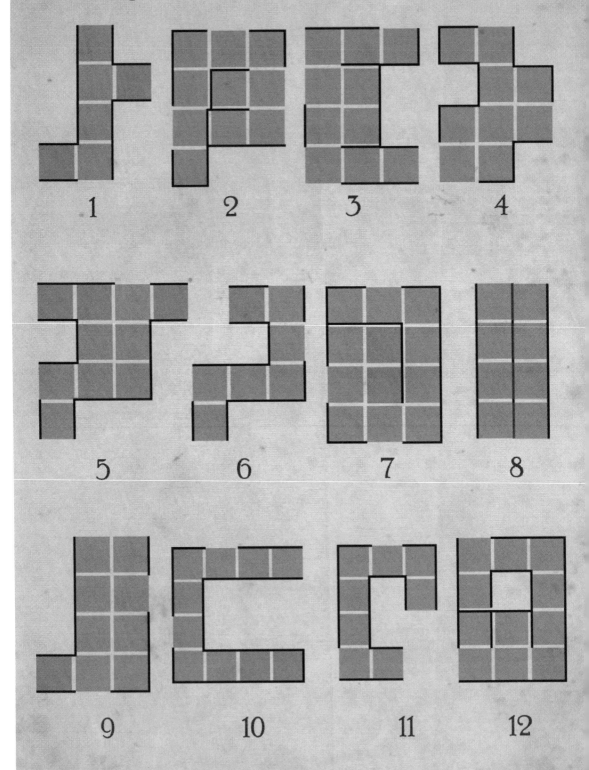

1D12 Dungeon Maze Sections

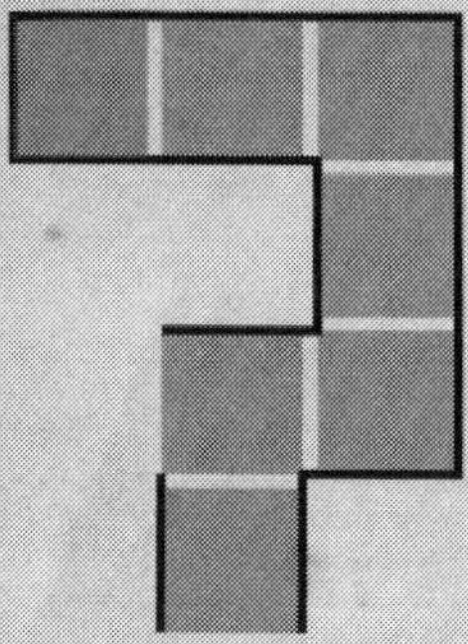

1

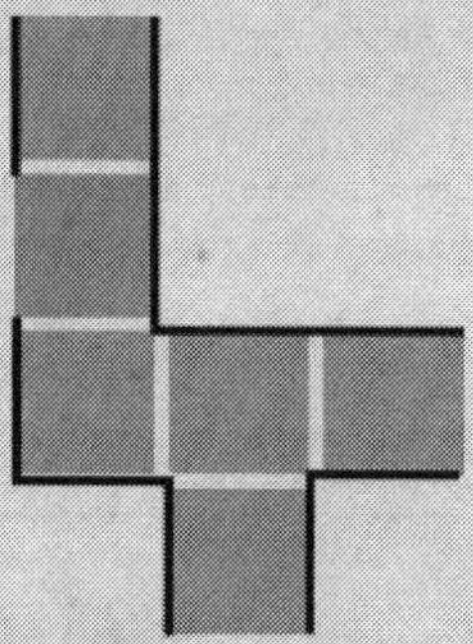

2

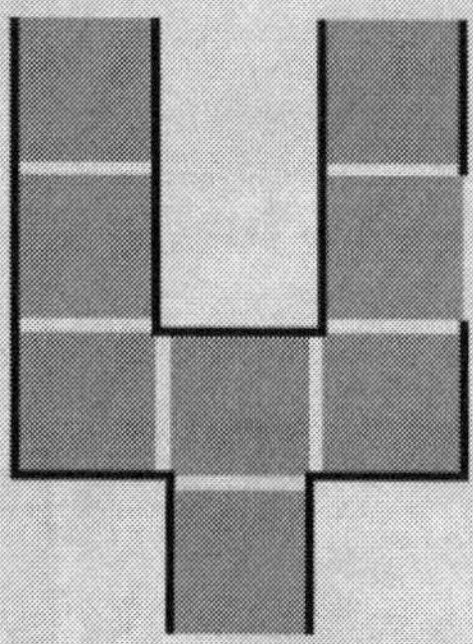

3

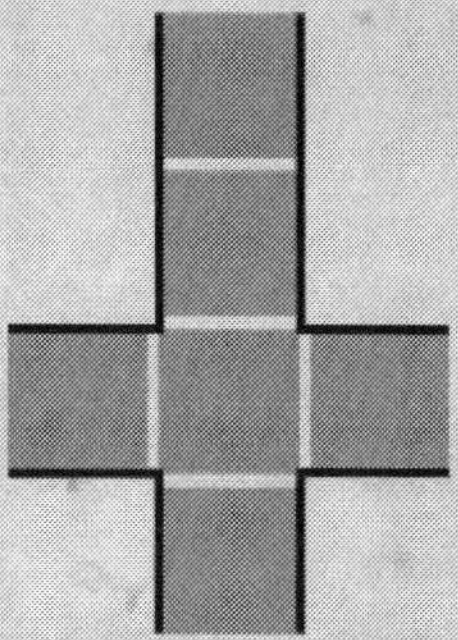

4

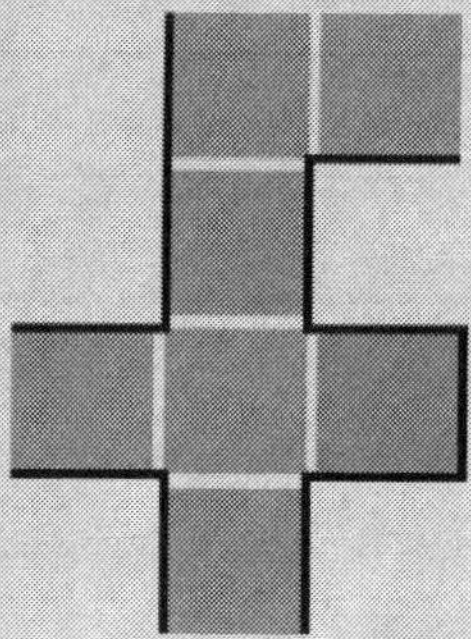

5

6

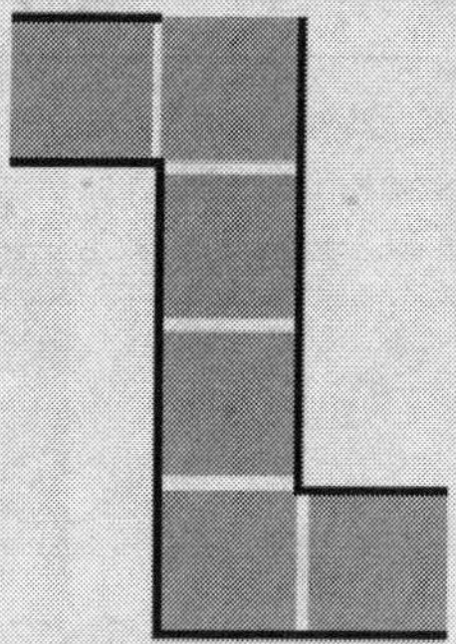

7

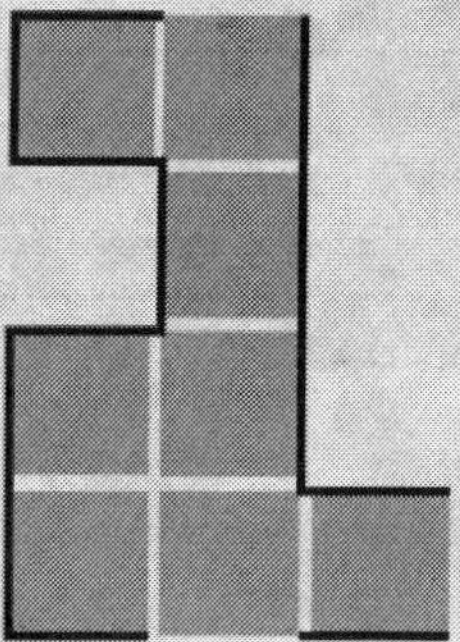

8

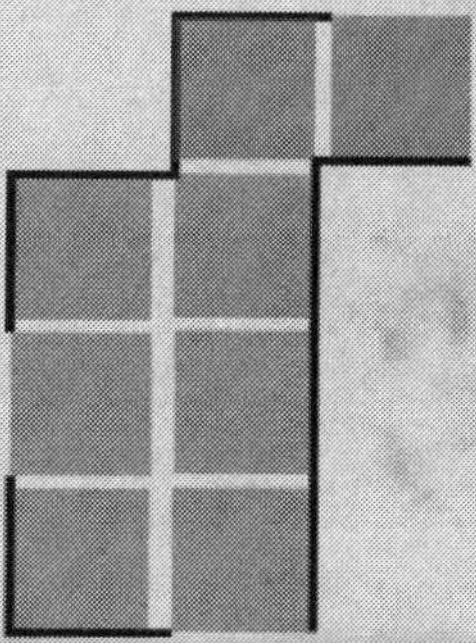

9

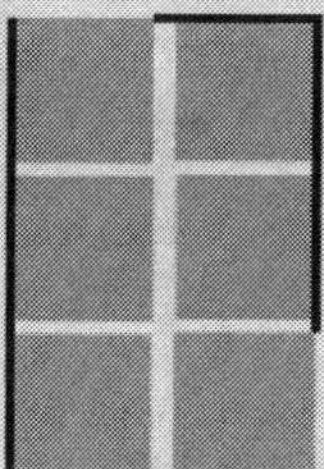

10

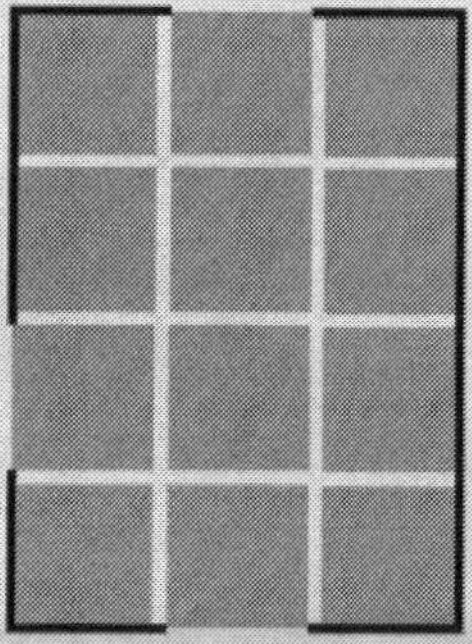

11

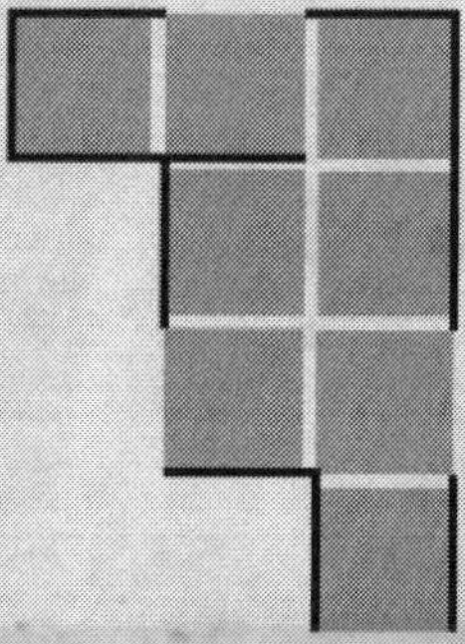

12

1D4 Crypt / Dungeon Chambers

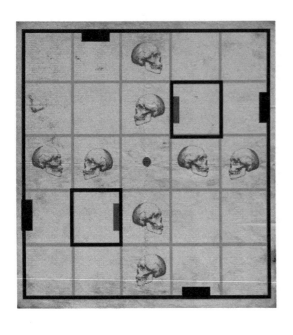

1

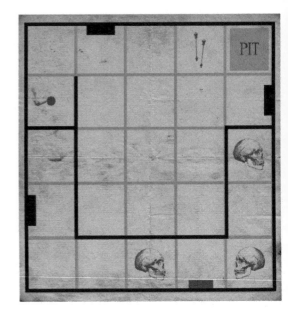

2

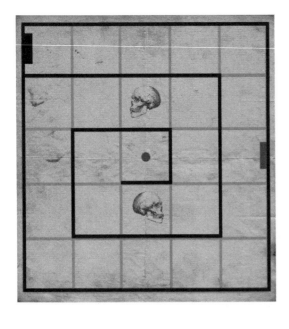

3

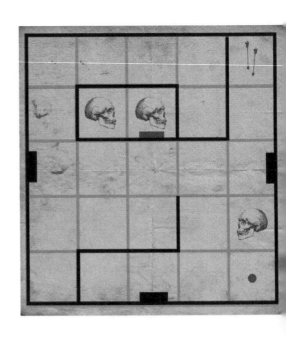

4

1D4 Crypt / Dungeon Chambers

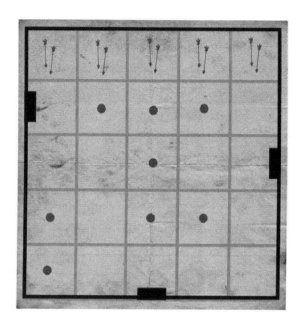

1

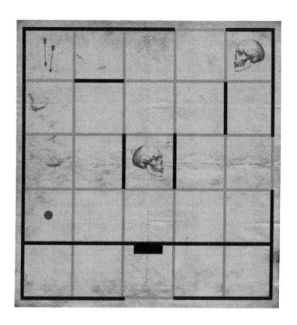

2

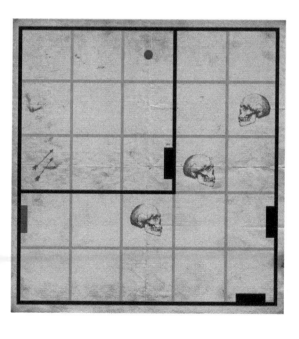

3

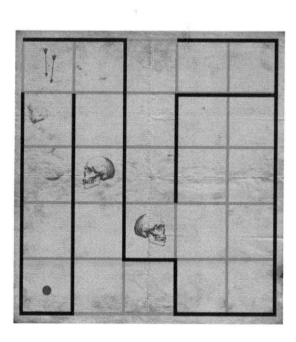

4

1D4 Crypt / Dungeon Chambers

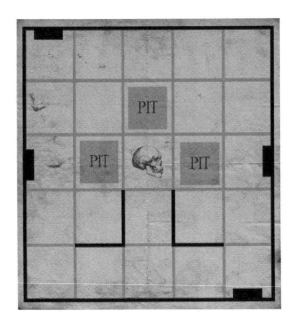

1

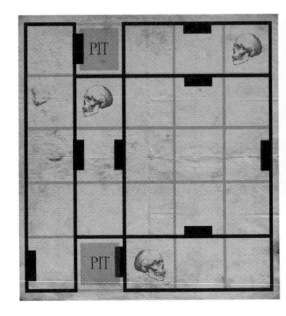

2

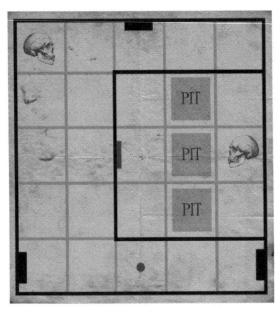

3

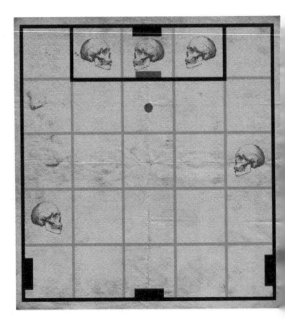

4

1D4 Crypt / Dungeon Chambers

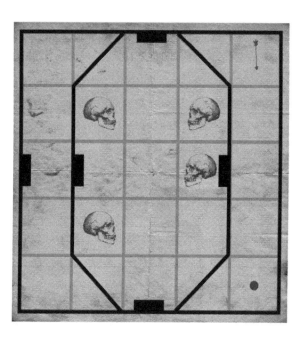

1

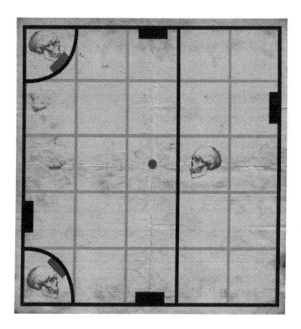

2

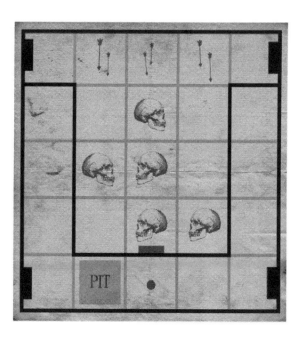

3

4

1D4 Crypt / Dungeon Chambers

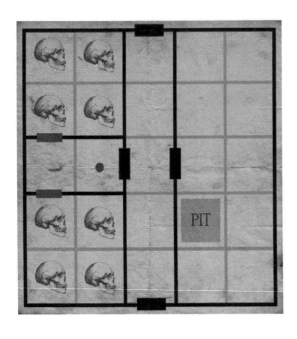

1

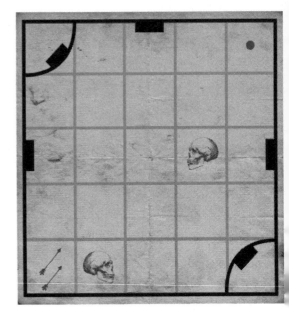

2

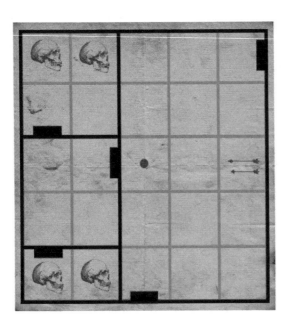

3

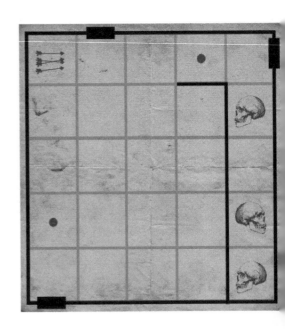

4

1D6 Dwellings

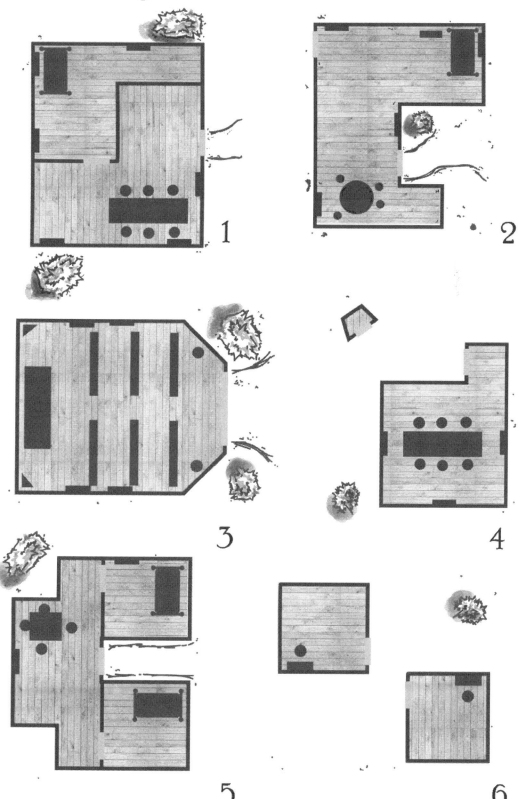

1D6 Dwellings

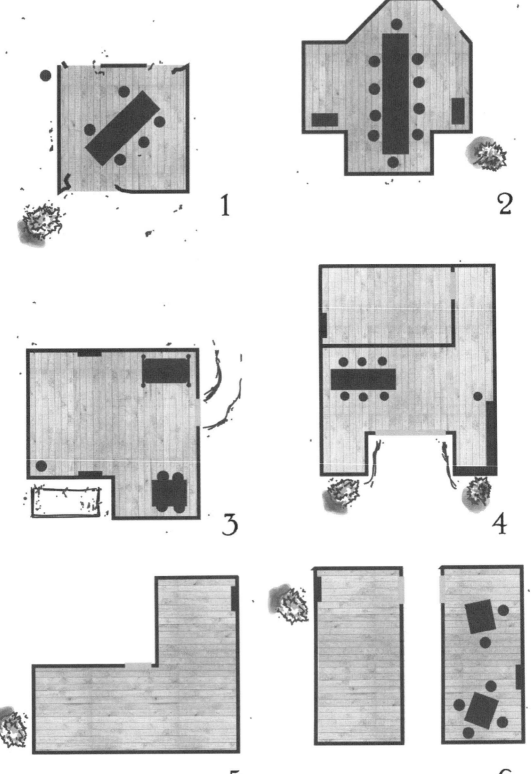

1D6 Dwellings

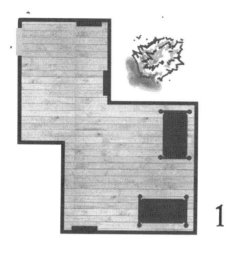

1

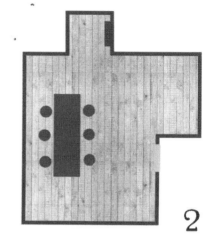

2

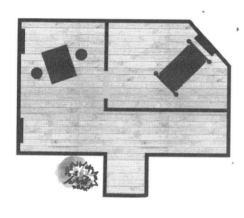

3

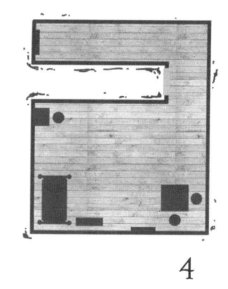

4

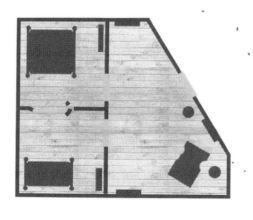

5

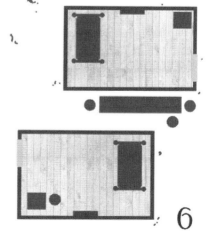

6

1D6 Dwellings

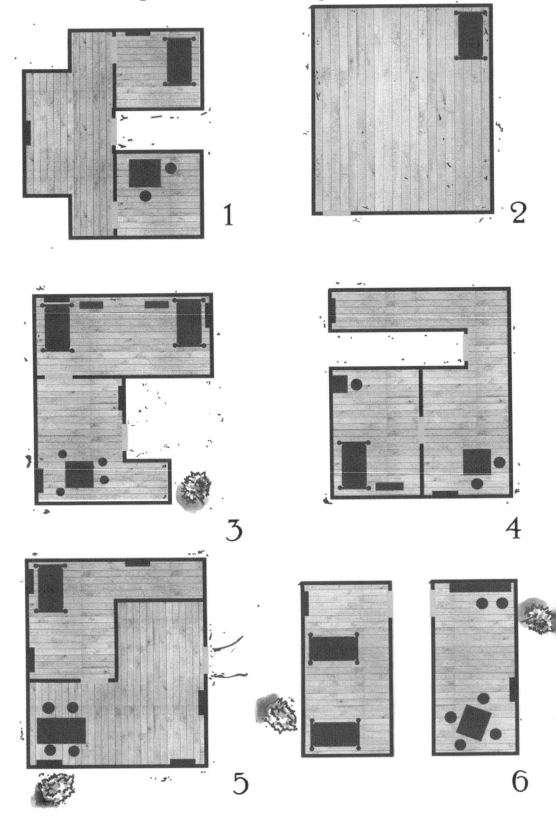

1

2

3

4

5

6

1D6 Dwellings

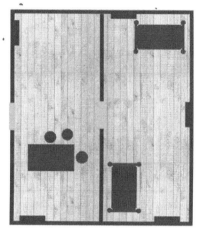

1

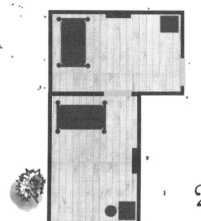

2

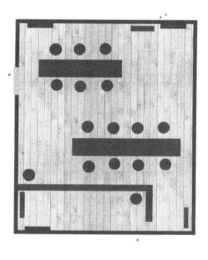

3

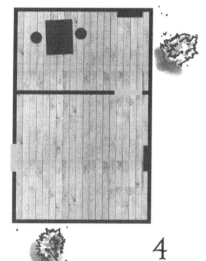

4

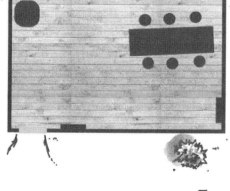

5

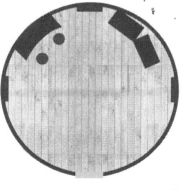

6

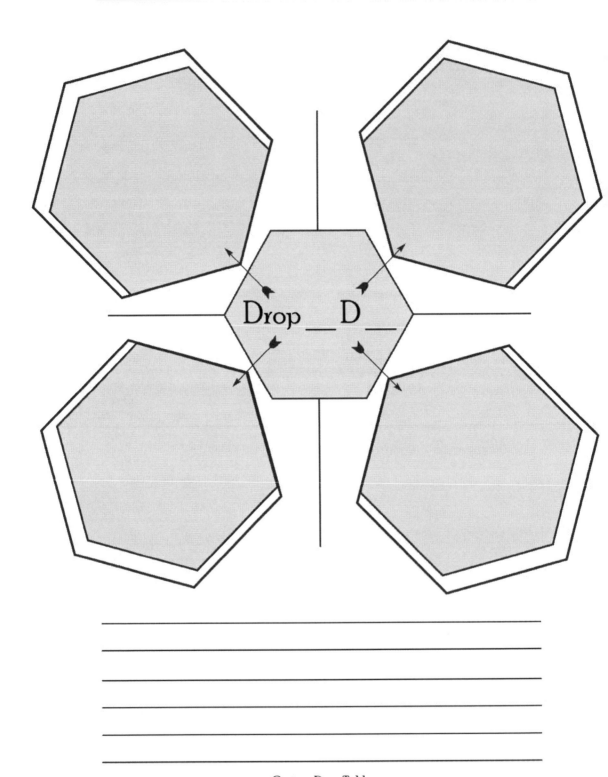

Custom Drop Table

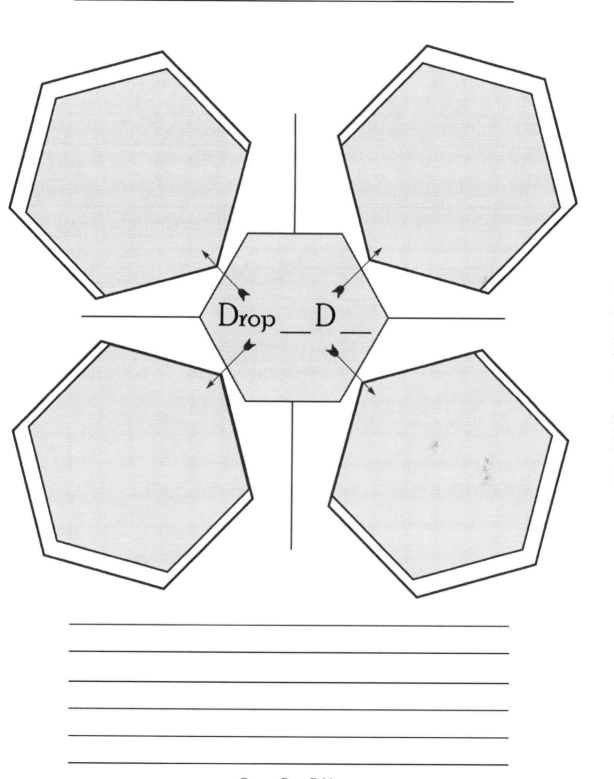

Custom Drop Table

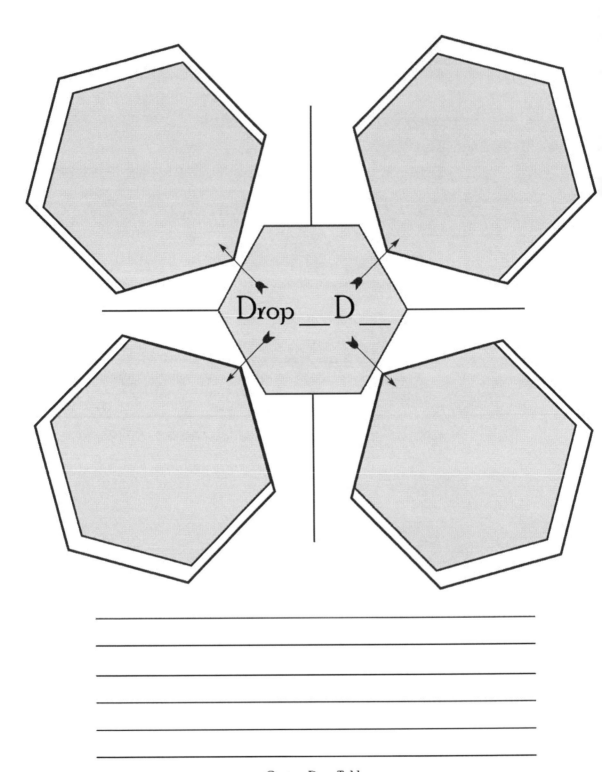

Drop ___ D ___

Custom Drop Table

_____

Drop __ D __

_____
_____
_____
_____
_____
_____

Custom Drop Table

Symbols for Locations

⬡ _____

⬡ _____

⬡ _____

⬡ _____

⬡ _____

⬡ _____

⬡ _____

⬡ _____

⬡ _____

⬡ _____

⬡ _____

⬡ _____

⬡ _____

Symbols for Locations

All text and artwork by Justin Sirois

Cover by Luke Eidenschink

SeveredBooks.com

The Party Backstory Generator is a collaborative
storytelling supplement that's a helluva lot of
fun for you and your players. It's sort of like a
workbook from your college lab class in that
you get to draw out the starting region for your
campaign, but everyone gets to collaborate and
add their own touch so your whole group is
invested in the setting. This book is a fun improv
exercise that will get your group off to a great
new start.

LUKE GYGAX

59449906R00079

Made in the USA
Columbia, SC
04 June 2019